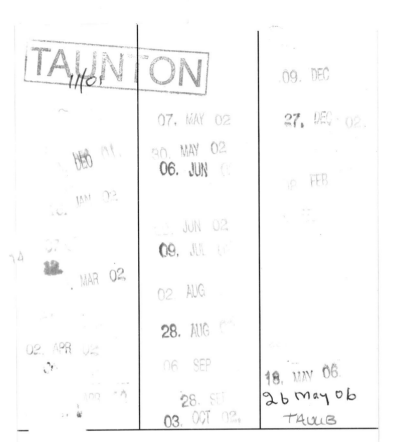

THE TOBRUK RESCUE

Further Titles by Duncan Harding from Severn House

ATTACK NEW YORK!
COME HELL OR HIGHWATER!
TORPEDO BOAT
FLOTILLA ATTACK
OPERATION CHARIOT
OPERATION JUDGEMENT
THE TOBRUK RESCUE
TUG-OF-WAR

Writing as Leo Kessler

S.S. WOTAN SERIES

ASSAULT ON BAGHDAD
FLIGHT FROM BERLIN
FLIGHT OVER MOSCOW
FIRE OVER SERBIA
OPERATION LONG JUMP
THE HITLER WEREWOLF MURDERS
S.S. ATTACKS

Writing as Charles Whiting

THE COMMON SMITH VC SERIES

THE BALTIC RUN
IN TURKISH WATERS
DEATH ON THE RHINE
PASSAGE TO PETROGRAD

Non-Fiction

PATHS OF DEATH AND GLORY

THE TOBRUK RESCUE

Duncan Harding

SEVERN SH HOUSE

This first world edition published in Great Britain 1995 by
SEVERN HOUSE PUBLISHERS LTD of
9–15 High Street, Sutton, Surrey SM1 1DF.
First published in the USA 1995 by
SEVERN HOUSE PUBLISHERS INC., of
595 Madison Avenue, New York, NY 10022.

British Library Cataloguing in Publication Data
Harding, Duncan
　Tobruk Rescue
　I. Title
　823.914 [F]

　ISBN 0-7278-4800-3

Typeset by Palimpsest Book Production Limited,
Polmont, Stirlingshire
Printed and bound in Great Britain by
Hartnolls Ltd, Bodmin, Cornwall.

"They speak of murder . . . I can't trust anyone any more. Assassination awaits me on the least suspicion."

Felix Stidger, Union spy, 1864

Book One

A Mission is Proposed

"The officer in charge must execute them at once. We cannot risk endangering the great secret."

Churchill to Field Marshal Sir Alan Brooke,
June 1942

ONE

The heat was intense. The sun struck like a sharp knife across the eyes. But the three men crouched around the radio set in the sand did not notice the heat or the harsh glare of the desert sun. They stared intently across the sparkling, rippling blue of the Mediterranean, watching the black dot as it grew larger and larger.

"*Was meinst du, Heinz?*" one said, squinting his eyes beneath the battered peaked cap of the Afrika Korps. "*Ein Tommy?*"

Heinz, his skinny arms covered with festering desert sores, for they had been out in the desert for seven days now without medical attention and little water, licked his cracked parched lips and said slowly, "*Ein Tommy.*"

The radioman wasted no further time. He picked up the mouthpiece and started reporting at once. "*Otto Eins . . . Otto Eins . . . bitte kommen . . . Otto Eins . . .*" And on the horizon the two-engined Wellington bomber started to make its descent.

The pilot spoke into the intercom. "All right Blue . . . Chalky . . . keep yer eyes skinned. I'm going down now."

"Like the proverbial tin of peeled tomatoes," Chalkey White, the mid-turret gunner, answered cheekily and spun his turret round so that the twin Browning machine guns

3

faced inland, the direction they would come from if they came. The pilot wiped the sweat from his tough bronzed face and pushed the stick forward.

Behind him in the rough canvas and leather seat, Dr Challenger put his bearded face closer to Dr Stein's pretty face and yelled above the roar of the engines, "The pilot told me before we took off this is the tricky bit, Lisa. With Tobruk surrounded, the Hun has got his people all round the port watching for anything coming in – ship or plane – or going out for that matter."

Lisa Stein paled a little under her tan and said in that heavily accented, but delightful voice of hers, "You mean, Professor, the enemy might attack us?"

Professor Dr Challenger stroked his thick black beard and throwing back his head, let out a great roar. "They wouldn't dare," he snorted. "Attack old Lost World Challenger? Not even the Hun would have such temerity."

Lisa Stein smiled. Her boss was obviously well aware of the nickname his students had called him by after the character in H. G. Wells' *Lost World*. Out of curiosity she had read the book soon after she had escaped from Germany and had been offered her post in London University's Department of Geology. After she had read the thriller, she had been forced to agree that there was some sort of similarity between H. G. Wells' fictional character and her boss. They were both big, heavy men with short fuses, who did not suffer fools gladly. Yes, Challenger had earned his old student nickname all right.

"Here they come, skipper," Blue yelled over the intercom. "Two of the bastards – *Messerchmitts!*"

The Australian pilot flung a hasty glance over his shoulder. Two yellow shapes were dropping out of the brilliant blue sky at a tremendous rate and they were closing up on the Wellington fast.

"Holy cow!" he cried angrily in the same instant that the mid-turret gunner opened fire. Suddenly the fuselage was flooded with the acrid stink of burned cordite. Empty cartridge cases started to tumble to the floor. Lisa Stein gasped with shock and Professor Challenger put his big hairy hand over hers reassuringly. "It's all right," he said soothingly. "They won't— "

He never finished his sentence. Suddenly a line of holes appeared the length of the fabric. Tiny fires broke out immediately. The pilot banked wildly and the great yellow shape of the Messerschmitt whizzed over their heads at 400mph.

Now the Wellington was skimming the surface of the sea. Its props stirred the water in wild fury. Challenger guessed that the pilot thought this was the best tactic to use against the much faster German fighters. If they made just one tiny mistake in their approach, they'd go straight into the sea.

"Bandit – to port!" Chalky White the Second gunner sang out over the intercom.

Again the harassed, sweat-lathered pilot chanced a look over his shoulder. He groaned. It was obvious that this was no hotshot just out of flying school. The German pilot was obviously very skilled. For he had lowered his undercarriage to reduce his speed drastically so that he was flying just above stalling speed. Now he was poising for a nice deflection shot.

The pilot acted instinctively. He jerked back the stick with all his strength, hoping that the Wellington was as tough as they were supposed to be. Every rivet, every joint in the plane seem to groan. The fabric shrieked.

But in the same moment that the German fired, the Wellington started to rise, the enemy tracer streaming harmlessly beneath it to pepper the sea.

It was the chance the mid-turret gunner had been waiting for. The Messerschmitt was only 150 yards away and flying at no more than 100 mph. He pressed his trigger, crying, "Try that one on for size, you frigging squarehead!"

The Messerschmitt staggered as if it had just run into an invisible wall. The perspex of the canopy crumbled into a glittering spider's web of broken glass. In a flash, thick white smoke started to stream from the fighter's shattered engine. Suddenly – startlingly – its painted nose tilted. The gunner caught a glimpse of the pilot's horrified face, with the blood streaming down it beneath the leather helmet, then he was gone, plunging straight into the sea.

"You got the bugger!" the pilot yelled excitedly. "Knock him for six . . . right out of the frigging sky."

Professor Challenger pressed Lisa's hand even harder and forced a tough smile. "Didn't I tell you. No Hun would dare to tackle old Lost— "

The words died on his lips, as a vicious burst of fire ran the length of the Wellington's port wing. Fuel started to stream out of the shattered engine immediately. The Wellington dropped alarmingly to one side. Frantically the pilot wrestled with the controls, cursing madly to himself as he tried to save the plane. But even as he did so, he knew it was no use. The plane was out of control and in half a minute the petrol escaping from the port engine would probably ignite. He made a snap decision. They were too low to parachute. Besides by the time the two VIPs got their 'chutes on they'd be falling out of the sky. "I'm going to ditch her!" he cried wildly over the intercom. "We're for the drink . . . Chalky look after the VIPs— "

Another angry burst of tracer slammed into the crippled Wellington. The plane shuddered violently. Lisa Stein cried out. Challenger half rose to his feet, his head almost touching the ceiling. He flashed a look through the porthole. Thick smoke was pouring out of the port engine. Already greedy little spurts of blue flame were starting up where the petrol was draining from the shattered engine. "Hold on," he commanded. "We're going down. Just stay close to me, Lisa. You'll be all right."

The Messerschmitt came in for the final sortie. Challenger could see it quite plainly as it came hurtling in, cannon thudding away in its wings. Tracer came spurting towards them like glowing golf balls.

The mid-turret gunner, who had spun its turret round so that he could drop into the plane and help the two VIPs, screamed shrilly. He fell on to the cartridge-littered floor. Lisa screamed too. The man's face was dripping on to his bullet-shattered chest like scarlet sealing wax. Even as he bent to help, Challenger knew that the gunner was dead. Lisa began to sob hysterically. Challenger spun round on her, eyes blazing with fury in that look that had terrified many an undergraduate who hadn't answered his questions fast enough in an oral examination. "Stop that . . . stop it *at once*!"

The pretty young lecturer continued to sob, her shoulders heaving frantically like those of a heart-broken child.

Challenger didn't hesitate. He slapped her – hard.

She gasped. "Why— "

"Shut up!" he interrupted her brutally. "We're going

to ditch. This is what you do. Bend you head, hands in front of your face, knees raised. Now come on – quick about it!"

The slap had had its effect. She bent her head and protected that pretty face of hers with her hands. He caught a quick glimpse of white legs, and told himself that there was no time for that kind of sexual nonsense now. They were fighting for their lives. He flung himself down beside her and did the same, though, with one mighty, hairy paw he kept hold of her protectively.

Just in time. With a great splash, the crippled bomber struck the water. The pilot reeled back under the impact. Next instant he gave a shriek of absolute pain as the wheel broke and shaft thrust its way through his body like a spear. Next instant he died, neatly skewered to his own seat.

Abruptly all was silent. In the distance, the surviving Messerchmitt did a great defiant victory roll over Tobruk and then zoomed away to its base at Benghazi. Nothing stirred in the crashed bomber as it floated on the surface of the Mediterranean. It was as if they were frozen like this for eternity.

Challenger broke the silence with a gasp of relief. Gently he released Lisa from his massive grip and said quite softly – for him – "Come on, young woman. We'd better get out of this crate before it goes under." He pulled out the small geologist's hammer which he carried with him everywhere (his students had often joked before the war that "old Lost World probably takes it to bed with him") and with one great heave ripped a hole in the fabric above his head. Another massive blow and he had broken away half a dozen of the Wellington's wooden struts so that now the hole was big enough for a person to get through.

"Out you go," he ordered. He picked up the woman as if she were a doll, lifted her through the hole, catching another glimpse of those delectable firm white thighs, and deposited her on the outside of the floating plane. "Just lie there," he commanded. "Don't make any movements. With a bit of luck, we'll float long enough for someone to spot us and pick us up. I'll see to the crew."

But already he knew as he fought his way through the shattered debris to the rear of the plane that the third crew member was either dead or seriously injured. He would have stirred by now if he wasn't.

Challenger was right. The third man, a boy really with too long hair, lay face downwards on the deck, his back ripped open by cannon shells, so that the shattered bones glistened like polished ivory in the red welter of blood and gore. "Poor chap," Challenger said sadly, then realising that time was running out, he heaved himself effortlessly through the hole and lay there blinking for a few moments in the sudden glare.

About a mile away, a Sunderland flying boat started to rise in the sky.

Lisa turned carefully and looked at him enquiringly.

He shook his big head and then looked at the city on the coast ahead, smoke coming up from the burning petrol dumps, with the German guns pounding the trenches in the outskirts of the port, while in the harbour itself, the masts of scores of wrecked ships poked up above the waterline.

"That's Tobruk," he said, noting the first white bow wave of the motorboat steering and ziz-zagging on its way to rescue them. "Been under siege by Rommel for weeks now. Wonder when—" he stopped abruptly as he realised for the first time the mess that they were in. Two top scientists, one of them German Jewish, possessed of the greatest secret of World War Two, trapped in a doomed garrison. "Christ," he muttered using the old phrase of the trenches when he had been a 17-year-old infantryman, *now we're really in the shit!*

TWO

Churchill sat up and stopped wallowing in his bath. He looked like a toothless pink Buddha, the soapy water dripping down his hairless pale chest. In a glass next to the bath were his false teeth. In the other next to him was a large brandy and soda. In spite of the soap running down his pink face, he was smoking a large double Coronna.

"Field Marshal Sir Alan Brooke, sir," the flunkey announced, trying not to see the great man's naked body.

Churchill gave him a toothless smile. The working class, he told himself, were always so inhibited about nakedness. "Show him in, Graves," he lisped, waving the big cigar like a baton.

"Would you like me to get a towel, sir, or something?" the valet ventured.

"Course not," Churchill rounded on him stoutly. "Do you think a field marshal of the King Emperor's army has never seen a naked man before? If my memory serves me rightly a great number of them have slept with naked men. Show him in. I can't waste this precious hot water." He snorted at his own humour and splashed some more water over his fat belly.

Brooke came in, looking as sour and as disapproving as ever. Churchill looked up at the bird-watching Ulsterman,

11

who was his Chief of the General Staff. "Well, Brookie," he demanded, knowing that the nickname always irritated the field marshal, "what brings you to me at this time of the morning? Your soldiers haven't started to fight, have they?" It was an unkind cut but Churchill meant it. He didn't think the British Army was fighting as bravely and as boldly as it should do. In the last three years since war had broken out in 1939 the British Army had suffered too many defeats and disasters.

Brooke's dark face flushed a little. He took the cut personally. Now he gazed down disapprovingly at the naked Churchill with his brandy and soda and fat cigar, although it was only 9.30 in the morning. He said, "Bad news, Prime Minister. Tobruk."

Churchill took the cigar out of his toothless mouth in a flash. "What about Tobruk?" he demanded harshly. "It hasn't fallen, has it?"

"No sir, not yet."

Churchill heaved a sigh of relief. "Thank God for that. My poor old body can't stand very many more shocks. Crete, Hong Kong, Singapore . . . They've all fallen to the enemy, one after another, like a set of dominoes."

Brooke nodded but said nothing. A year before the Australians had held out in a besieged Tobruk for months on end. They had beaten Rommel, the "Desert Fox", as the damned Press was calling him, as if he were some damned film star, into the ground. Now the Libyan port was being held by the South Africans and he didn't think they had the same staying power as the "diggers".

"Well," Churchill demanded, puffing again at his expensive cigar, "pray enlighten me."

Suddenly, Brooke, who was usually unflappable, if dour, looked uneasy and anxious. He looked to left and

12

right, as if he thought he might be overheard. It's tube alloys, sir," he said in a whisper.

"*Tube alloys*," Churchill snorted, puzzled. Then it came to him, "Oh, my God. Has someone blabbed?"

"No, Prime Minister," Brooke answered promptly. "Not yet at least."

"But what role do tube alloys play in the defence of Tobruk?"

"None whatsoever, sir, save this. Professor Challenger and Dr Stein have been forced down there and are trapped in the port. If the Germans attack and capture Tobruk and the two of them are taken prisoner . . ." Brooke shrugged and didn't complete the rest of his sentence because there was no need to do so. Churchill would understand.

Slowly Churchill took the big cigar out of his mouth again as the full implications of what Brooke had just said dawned upon him. "The two civilians flew out to the Belgian Congo to check upon the uranium deposits there, didn't they. They are the most skilled geologists in the country, we were informed at the time."

"Exactly, sir. They were on their way back in stages. They'd fuelled up in Cairo and were flying the next leg of their journey to Gibraltar and from there back to Croydon to report. Now their plane has been downed at Tobruk."

Churchill considered for a moment or two, while Brooke cocked his head and listened intently, the crisis forgotten for a moment. He was sure he had just heard a warbler outside in the garden at Chequers.

"Do these people Challenger and – er Stein – know what tube alloys are?" Churchill asked.

Brooke forgot the warbler. "Yes, I'm afraid they do. Professor Challenger – a great big hulking bear of a fellow – is very direct. If I remember correctly, he asked straight

13

out why we were sending him out to the Belgian Congo in the middle of a war and at great expense and trouble to look over uranium deposits. We, therefore, had to make him swear and sign the Official Secrets Act. Then we told him that we needed the stuff for the production of the bomb. The Americans hadn't got enough of it in their own country."

Churchill's expression did not change. He said, "Give me that towel over there, please."

The Chief of the General Staff told himself a little angrily that the PM must think him a bloody servant or something. All the same, he handed Churchill the fluffy white towel, who began to rub at his genitals and belly with it thoughtfully. Brooke pulled a face at the sight and Churchill, as worried as he was, chuckled and said, "Never fear, Brookie, that particular pigeon is never going to fly again."

Brooke went red.

Churchill finished drying his lower body and then wrapping the big towel around he was serious once more. "Now then we must ensure that the two of them are brought out of Tobruk as quickly as possible. They must not fall into the hands of the Boche."

Brooke frowned. "It's going to be difficult, damnably difficult, Prime Minister," he said grimly. "Rommel has got Tobruk sewn up pretty tightly. I know the perimeter at Tobruk is pretty extensive, but he's got standing patrols everywhere, all linked by armoured cars. The Arabs are not to be trusted either. The Hun pays them for any of our chaps that they betray."

"By air?"

Brooke shook his head. "Virtually impossible. The only air strip has been bombed time and time again. We haven't

14

been able to get a plane in or out of Tobruk for nearly two weeks now."

"By sea?" Churchill persisted a little desperately.

Brooke hesitated for a moment. "The entrance to Tobruk harbour is mined and the harbour itself is well within the range of Rommel's artillery. Those 88s of his plaster anything trying to get in. However, Prime Minister, there is another small natural habour some twenty miles west of Tobruk. A very small craft could get in there and take the two of them off. The problem is, however, *how* to get them out of Tobruk in the first place." He sucked his prominent teeth thoughtfully.

"I take it, you don't trust the South Africans to do the job for you?" Churchill asked.

"No, quite frankly, PM, I don't. They seem to have lost the will to fight. Besides they have traitors among their ranks. Intelligence knows that for certain. In essence, therefore, it would be too risky to entrust the Springboks with getting our people out."

"What is your suggestion then?" Churchill asked and took a sip of his drink.

Brooke sniffed at the sight. It didn't seem right to him that the leader of the British Empire should be imbibing strong drinks at this time of the morning. But then, as he always told himself at such moments, Winston Spencer Churchill *was* a law unto himself. "We send in a long range desert group. You've heard of them Prime Minister?"

"Yes, they raid the Hun from their bases in the trackless desert. Hit and run chaps."

"Exactly. Well Prime Minister, I'm ordering one of the LRDG teams to try to sneak through Rommel's lines and into Tobruk. With a bit of luck, they'll get this Professor

15

Challenger out with the woman. Now we can't expect civilians to cross hundreds of miles of desert in the June heat to our own lines in Egypt. I suggest then that they take them to the little natural harbour I have just mentioned where they'll be picked up by one of our ships and taken straight to Malta."

"By submarine?"

"No, Prime Minister, the coastal waters are too shallow. A Hun aircraft would soon spot a sub, even if it were submerged, in those waters."

"I see," Churchill said after he had absorbed the information, "then it will have to be a surface craft."

"Yes, something inconspicuous that won't attract the attention of the Boche. There's an old naval tug, German-made by the way, so it can easily adopt a German identity for the crossing, at Malta. It's called the *Black Swan*. We'd use that."

Churchill laughed, revealing his toothless pink gums. "You know what they call ships named the *Black Swan* in the Royal Navy, Brookie?"

"No, Prime Minister."

"I'll tell you. It's traditional. They call them the 'Mucky Duck'."

Field Marshal Sir Alan Brooke was not amused. He waited impatiently for Churchill's decision. There was trouble again in the Middle East. He wanted to get back to the War Office and find out the latest from Cairo.

Churchill spoke. "Yes, put that plan into action immediately, if you would. I have only one small addition to make, Brookie."

"What sir?"

Churchill's almost cherubic appearance changed suddenly. Even with the damp towel wrapped around his chubby figure and standing there in his bare feet, he looked frightening. "If there is any danger of this Challenger and the Stein woman being caught by the Hun, the officer in charge must execute them at once. We cannot risk endangering the great secret."

Brooke looked at the Prime Minister aghast. "Kill them in cold blood – and a woman, too. But sir," he stuttered.

Churchill raised his hand for silence. "There are no buts, Field Marshal. I have made my decision. They are to be killed. Now, if you won't stay for a drink – and I know you won't – I bid you goodbye." Churchill turned and wandered off into the bedroom, leaving wet footprints on the floor, and Field Marshal Sir Alan Brooke staring after him in complete and absolute disbelief.

Outside the warbler had ceased singing.

THREE

Cairo was in one hell of a flap. As the gharri left the station, Hard could see the line of frightened European civilians jostling in their attempts to get on the next train to Palestine. There were hundreds of British soldiers, too, rifles slung over their shoulders, their hair bleached to tow, looking browned off with the heat, the war and the "Gippos". Their every gesture seemed to reveal their resentment of their lot and their fear, too, because all of them knew they'd soon be going "up the blue", as they called the Desert, once more to meet Rommel and his damned panzers.

Once the gharri was stopped by an Egyptian policeman wearing a fez to allow a general in a staff car go by and Hard watched as a young British soldier knocked over a basket of fruit proferred by an Egyptian hawker, crying as he did so, "Bugger off, you dirty sodding Gippo bugger!" As the hawker, near to tears, bent to pick up his precious fruit, the soldier ground his boot savagely into it. Then he stomped off, hands deep in the pockets of his shorts. Behind him the hawker spat into the white choking dust and hurled a stream of guttural Arabic after him.

On the seat of the gharri, Hard smiled, as the hawker suddenly lifted up his dirty robe to reveal his penis and cry, "Soon you will be running fast for the Nile, English dog. Then I fuck your women for you."

The worried gharri driver turned and saw the look on the English major's lean, bronzed face. "You understand, *Effendi?*" he asked in Arabic.

Hard nodded. "Yes, I understand all right. Though I think if he was wise, he wouldn't want to fuck English women. Well, not the kind you find in Cairo."

The driver flicked his whip and the old nag drawing the carriage moved forward again, the bells on its harness jingling weakly, as if they, too, just like the skinny-ribbed nag, were lacking in strength to do more.

Hard went into the mess first for a drink. He had been longing for an ice-cold Rheingold beer for six weeks now, ever since they had set out into the desert for another raid on Rommel's flanks. He knew his orders were to report immediately, but Hard had never taken orders literally. That's why he had volunteered for the Long Range Desert Group back in 1941.

The bar was packed with staff officers in their elegant gabardine uniforms, downing gins and tonic and automatically waving their fly whisks although there wasn't a fly to be seen. He ordered the beer from the mess servant in his starched white jacket and listened to gossip and chatter around him. The "staff wallahs" were obviously in the same kind of flap as the rest of Cairo's foreign population. The chatter was full of talk of burning documents, sending "the little woman" by the next train to Palestine, the generals who already had their bags packed and the "insolent damned Gippos" who kept pointing to the bronze-brown kites, Cairo's scavengers, and jeering "They'll be waiting for you when the air raids start *Effendi.*"

Hard looked at the reflections of their well-fed, flabby

faces in the big mirror behind the bar in disgust. Here, there was defeatism in the very air. How could they expect the men of the Eighth Army who were "up the blue" doing the fighting to win when they, the staff, were already planning to do a bunk? For a moment he was tempted to down another Rheingold. Then he thought better of it. It wouldn't do to report to the general, smelling too much of beer. He smiled at his own almost emaciated face in the mirror, signed the chit and went out.

They kept him waiting in the great echoing entrance hall to the GHQ. But he was used to that. The staff always kept line officers waiting, however urgent their business. Perhaps it was policy, Hard thought to himself, a way of keeping frontline officers in their place.

Again there were signs of the big flap all around him. Dispatch riders, covered in dust, bearing leather pouches, came and went hastily. Young staff officers, with worried faces, came by whispering. From an open door bearing the old poster warning "Keep Mum", a high-pitched voice, bordering on the hysterical, was saying, "But I've already told you, sir. One of our patrols spotted some Boche officers poking the sand of the Great Depression with their sticks. Obviously, sir, they were testing whether it would bear the weight of their tanks. And once they're across the Great Depression, sir, we're for the ruddy high jump."

Hard shook his head in disgust in the same instant that an immaculate staff captain, all pressed starched khaki uniform and gleaming Sam Brown cross-belt, approached him and said, "Major Hard?"

Hard rose to his feet. "Yes, I'm Hard, Captain."

The young staff captain looked at the lean, hawk-nosed officer in his worn khaki and with those fierce challenging blue eyes of his and told himself *"nomen es omen"*. Hard by name and hard by looks. Then he said, "The General will see you now, sir."

The General was unlike anyone else Hard had met so far in Cairo. He was small, had a tough face like a bulldog – and a voice to match it – and the dull red of the Victoria Cross decorated his chest. "Hard," he barked without preliminaries, "Got a job for your lot. Very important. The PM ordered it himself." He barked out the words in short harsh grunts, as if it would take far too much effort to form a longer sentence.

"Yessir," Hard answered automatically, a little bewildered by the little General's brisk impatient manner.

"No, you don't," the General contradicted him sharply. He tapped the big brown envelope on the desk in front of him and now Hard noticed that two of his fingers had been shot away at some time or other. "Those are your detailed orders, but you'll only open them when you're safely back in the desert with your unit. Cairo's full of damned spies and gippos just waiting for the Hun to *liberate* them." His face twisted in scorn. "Half the damned Egyptian Army's in their pay. It was only the other day that we nabbed their Chief of Staff trying to do a bunk to the Hun. No matter." He controlled himself with difficulty. "Now, in brief. You've got to get into Tobruk. Two damned silly civilians have got themselves trapped there. You've got to get them out."

"We can get them out, sir. That's no problem But we *couldn't* get them back. Untrained civilians couldn't stand several hundred miles across the desert. Little water and the heat— "

The General held up the hand with the missing fingers for silence. He smiled. To Hard it looked as if his jaws

21

were worked by tight springs. He told himself he wouldn't like to work permanently for the little general. "Who said anything about taking them back across the desert, eh? You— " The General stopped short. He frowned.

"You can't come in here like that!" the immaculate young staff captain was protesting outside the General's door. "I mean— "

"Shut yer gob," a rough Yorkshire voice cut in crudely. "I've bin ordered here. So here I am to see the frigging general." The next moment the door was flung open. A burly man in a battered blue naval uniform staggered in and for a moment Hard thought he might well keel over. Even at that distance he could smell the reek of whisky.

He looked at the elderly naval lieutenant, with a face that looked as if it had been hewn out of granite, and then back to the little General. He waited for the explosion to come. It didn't. Instead the General said quite pleasantly – for him, "You'll be Lieutenant Christian of the *Black Swan*."

"Ay," the Yorkshireman growled and looked at the General suspiciously, as if wondering why he was not being hauled over the coals for his insolent behaviour.

Quickly the General introduced the two of them and Hard blanched as he smelled the whisky on Christian's breath as the latter squeezed his hand in his own hard paw. He had seen some hard men in his time and he guessed that Christian was one of them. He noted, too, that the sailor bore the ribbons of the DSO and DSC as well as those of the First World War, on the breast of his dirty wrinkled tunic.

"Well, gentlemen, I'm not going to take up any more of your precious time. You're to share a little house in the

22

compound where you can discuss your plans undisturbed and in privacy. You'll have twenty-four hours. Give me a one-sheet outline. I'll forward it to the War Office. Remember this is very hush-hush indeed." Then the little General looked at Hard and said, "Oh by the way, Hard, this is your transport for the way back." Then he actually winked . . .

"This is the place," the elegant staff captain said, as he clambered out of the jeep, carefully keeping to windward of the naval officer who had swigged whisky straight from his hip flask all the time during their drive to the compound. "You can see it's well guarded. The General's orders."

Hard was impressed. In contrast to the slackness of GHQ, here there was purpose, order and discipline. On the flat roof of the two-storey, white-painted house, a MP with a bren gun was positioned in a circle of sandbags. Two others were in sandbagged positions on either side of the entrance and at the door itself, a hard-faced redcap, with a tommy gun tucked purposefully beneath his right arm, stood waiting for them.

"What's this then?" Christian growled as the redcap officer stamped his boot down hard and saluted, "the ruddy royal palace?"

"No sir," the redcap snapped back crisply, "Just the secure compound." The General's ordered you a permanent twenty-four-hour guard as long as you're in Cairo. Can't be too careful, sir." He stamped his foot down again and gave them a hard-faced smile.

Christian sniffed. "I think I need another drink." He took out the flask, shook it and pulled a face. It was empty.

"There's a bottle of locally made Victory Scotch

whisky on the sideboard inside," the staff captain volunteered. "Not very good, I'm afraid."

"It's whisky, isn't it," Christian growled and, elbowing the MP officer to one side, he lurched hurriedly into the house, as if he couldn't get to the whisky fast enough.

The staff captain shrugged a little helplessly and Hard grinned. He could see he was going to have his hands full with Lieutenant Peter Christian. The staff captain fled.

"Let's get this straight, if we're going to work together," Christian said five minutes later. "I'm an awkward bugger. Always have been. That's why I'm still a first lieutenant after three years of war and in command of that old tub – the 'Mucky Duck' – *Black Swan* to you. But I'll tell you one thing." He pointed a forefinger like a hairy sausage at Hard. "I know my job. I've been at sea since I was sixteen. Thirty years of it, Navy and Merchant Navy. Oh, and yes, I drink." He downed the hald tumbler of local-made firewater as if it were orange juice. "Now tell me about yersen." He refilled his glass.

"Regular," Hard said, feeling that he was going to like Christian – for all his failings. He came to the point straightway and he liked direct men. He had long learned that in this war, there was no time for niceties. You lost battles like that. "Straight into the Guards from Sandhust in 1939. Wounded in France in '40. Got put in the bag in Greece in late '40. Did a bunk and was posted to the Western Desert. Volunteered for the Long Range Desert Groups in '41. Been with them ever since."

"That makes you about twenty-five."

Hard nodded.

"You look older," Christian growled and took another mighty slug of the firewater. "All right, I think we're

24

gonna to get on. But none of that Regular Army bull with me. I won't wear it."

"You won't have to," Hard agreed and then said hastily, "All right, Christian, let's get on with it. This is the drill."

"I'm all frigging ears," Christian said, hand on his tumbler. But this time he didn't drink . . .

FOUR

"I should have bloody well known," the redcap captain moaned, holding a shell dressing, already scarlet with his blood, to his wounded head. "I thought I knew all those sodding Gippo tricks, but they really caught me with my knickers down."

It was evening. Hard and Christian had just returned from the mess where they had eaten (and in Christian's case mostly drunk) their dinner.

Now the two of them looked around the "guarded compound" in dismay. The windows were splintered. Bullet marks pocked the walls and there was a dead redcap sprawled out in the rubble. Already the bells were jingling as the Army ambulances rushed to the site of the shooting.

"What happened?" Hard asked, instinctively touching his breast pocket where the secret orders the little General had given him rested. They were still there, thank God.

"Just as the sun was going down. You know what it's like out here? One minute it's light, the next it's pitch dark. A group of Gippos with donkeys, carrying carpets. You know the kind? Genuine Persian, made in the backstreets of Cairo. I had a dekko at them and told myself I know the type. First carpets, then dirty pictures and if you like they can arrange you a woman. All pink inside

26

like English lady." He mimicked the Egyptian sing-song bitterly.

Christian took out his hip flash, shook it to reassure himself there was plenty left for a stiff nightcap and offered the flask to the redcap. "Put one of those past yer tonsils," he growled.

Gratefully the wounded policeman took a sip, while Hard waited impatiently.

"One of them came up the path," the MP went on, "with a carpet over his arm. The duty man at the door told him to bugger off. Next moment there was all hell let loose. The Gippo dropped the carpet and started firing with a Tommy gun. One of the donkey wallahs flung a grenade and did for poor Corporal James on the bren and that started it. We let them have it." He indicated the dead donkeys sprawled out piteously in their own blood. "And they were bloody determined for Gippos. You know how they get the wind-up even if you just look at 'em. Well, this little lot didn't." The MP dabbed his bleeding forehead once more tenderly. "I'm certain they'd have done for the lot of us if the sirens hadn't started. Then they did a bunk 'cept those two." He indicated an Egyptian sprawled over the split sandbags where the dead redcap lay behind his shattered gun and another one crumpled in the door. "We got those buggers all— "

Hard indicated with a nod that he had heard enough in the same instant that the boxlike Army ambulance skidded to a stop. "Off you go and get yourself patched up. That head wound looks nasty. We'll look after ourselves for the rest of this night. Thank you."

Groaning a little now, the redcap limped over to the waiting stretcher-bearers, while Hard went over to the dead Egyptian sprawled in the doorway. The man was

27

big and brawny for an Egyptian and on a sudden impulse he pulled up the man's left sleeve, while Christian peered over his shoulder curiously in the shaft of yellow light coming from inside the shattered room.

Hard nodded. It confirmed the drift of his thoughts.

"Well?" Christian demanded.

"Don't you see," Hard pointed to the vaccination marks on the dead man's muscular arm.

"No."

"Those shot marks – and look at his feet." He pointed to the Egyptian's dusty feet.

Again Christian shook his head in bewilderment.

"Well, they're bare like all Gippo peasants' feet." He lifted the dead man's left foot. "They're soft underneath though but calloused at the toes."

"Now then, Hard, I'm no ruddy Sherlock Holmes, yer know. Get on with it, man."

Hard grinned in spite of the tension. "Well, I'll clue you in. This Gippo was no ordinary hawker. He's been vaccinated for one thing, and most peasants never even see a medic. He's been used to regular food and exercise. Look at that arm – plenty of meat and brawn on it. And he's been used to wearing shoes – or rather boots – for years."

Christian scratched his grizzled head in bewilderment.

"I'm still no bloody wiser than I was afore," he complained.

"This man was in the Army – the Gippo Army. Who else in Egypt would be trained to use a Tommy gun? And, as you've heard from the redcap, the average Gippo is not normally a very aggressive creature."

"All right, I see what you're meaning now. But still it doesn't add up to me, Hard."

28

"Well, they weren't obviously after the redcaps. What gain would they have from that?"

Christian whistled softly. "You mean they were after *us*?" he exclaimed.

"Exactly."

"But why?"

Hard frowned with exasperation. "I wish I knew," he said after a moment or two. "Obviously they know we're up to something."

"Who's *they*?" Christian interjected. "Spit it out."

"Those traitors in the Egyptian Army who . . ." he hesitated momentarily, then put his thoughts into words, "who are working hand-in-glove with the Jerries."

"So you mean the squareheads are on to us even before we get started?"

"Something like that, I'm afraid." He sucked his teeth thoughtfully. Then he said, "You know the plan now, Christian. I think our best bet is to go back to GHQ for the rest of this night. We'll be safer there."

"Yes."

"And then you start back for Malta in the morning and alert your – what do you call it?" He grinned suddenly.

"The 'Mucky Duck'," Christian growled and then for the first time since Hard had met him, he actually smiled, revealing a mouthful of yellow-stained teeth.

"Yes, the Mucky Duck for departure as soon as you receive our signal."

Christian nodded his understanding and asked, "How long do you think you'll take . . . to get in and out of Tobruk, I mean?"

"Come on, I'll show you," Hard answered. He walked back inside the battered house and over to the big map of the Western Desert on the wall, with a length of holes along it where it had taken a burst of Tommy gun fire. "Now this is the way to the back door into Libya. There are two of them in fact. You follow the route south-west past the Giza pyramids. Two days later you are at Ain Dulla. That's a small oasis on the eastern fringe of something called the Great Sand Sea. There you turn west where you face what one of the early explorers of the desert called the 'Easy Ascent.'" He indicated the point on the map which was virtually unmarked at that spot, signifying that area had not yet been properly explored.

Christian nodded his understanding and waited for Hard to continue, telling himself as he did so that Hard was a tough young man, if he was prepared to tackle an expedition of the kind he was proposing.

"The 'Easy Ascent' is a great curving ramp of sand running up to the summit of a rock wall. These days it's a bit of a mess because every three weeks one of our Long Range Desert Patrols go up it – and despite its name it isn't easy at all. But it can, naturally, be done."

Christian grunted something and stared at the white emptiness below the "Easy Ascent".

"Once you're through the narrow rock ridge between the two very deep gullies – here," Hard continued, "then you've reached the Great Sand Sea and the backdoor to Libya is open." He paused and then, speaking slowly, as if he were pondering the matter, he went on with, "There is another way, however." He pointed to the end of the Great Sand Sea, perhaps a hundred miles further south, deep into the desert. "Here – is the end of surveyed territory. But we do know out there, there is a mountain range. It might be passable because the rock would offer traction for the vehicles."

The Tobruk Rescue - The Route

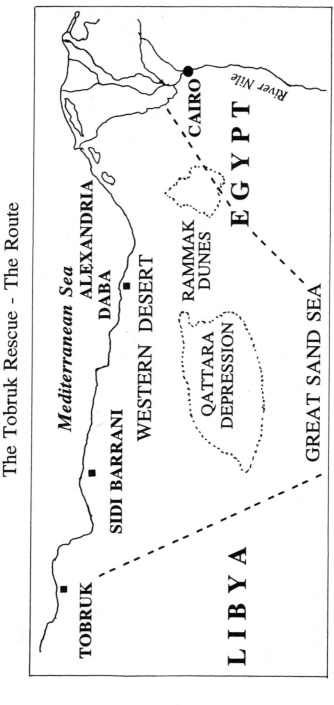

The Route– – – – –

31

"But how do you know?" Christian objected.

"Well, I've never been that far myself of course." Hard looked thoughtful. "But in 1937, the Anglo-Egyptian society did send out an expedition in order to survey the area. It was led by three men – an Egyptian, an English officer and a Hungarian – Count von Almaszy. The count had a bee in his bonnet about finding the lost oasis of Pharoah Canbyses, who went mad and disappeared into the desert in the fifth century before Christ. Now only the Hungarian came back. The others, he told people in Cairo, had died from heat stroke and thirst in the desert. Soon, thereafter, von Almaszy went to Germany." He shrugged. "Had he got through? We don't know. And if he had charted the route, again we wouldn't know. Because with the outbreak of war the Germans weren't obviously sending us any new maps."

"So," Christian said slowly, "I'm thinking you'll be taking that route."

"You read my mind."

"All right then, when do you want me in that little harbour?" Christian was very businesslike although he'd consumed another half a bottle of whisky over dinner.

Hard did a quick calculation. "Two weeks from tomorrow," he said after a moment's thought.

Christian nodded his understanding. "I'll be there," he said firmly. "You can rely on me and that old tub the Mucky Duck."

"I know I can," Hard stretched out his hand.

Christian took it in his own paw, squeezed hard and then said, "Now I think we've deserved a little drink."

"Just the job. Let's get over to GHQ and I'll buy you that – er – *little drink*."

The bond had been established.

FIVE

The Kit-Kat Club was packed. Every table of the night club was filled with drunken staff officers and whores from Alexandria, mostly French. The air was blue with smoke. Champagne corks popped. Waiters in red fezzes and long white robes ran back and forth with their silver trays. Cigarette girls in short skirts, wearing sheer black stockings, offered their wares winningly – and it wasn't only cigarettes they sold.

Colonel Wharton-Ware of GHQ was enjoying himself immensely. He had packed off the "memsahib" – with her directoire knickers and her constant chiding that "Archie, you've already had *it* once this month, surely you can't expect *it* again" – to Palestine at the beginning of the flap. Now he indulged in "it" every night, and would continue to do so until, as he told another staff officer, "We've got to make a run for it, old boy, what?"

Squeezed in between Yvonne and Carla, both half his age, but very willing, he watched the undulations of the plump Egyptian belly dancer in a drunken haze, but with a great deal of sexual anticipation. Each time she thrust out her pelvis and gave that peculiar grunt they all made, he could have had one of the two whores there and then right across the table. Yvonne was already helping him too. Her cunning little fingers were already unbuttoning his flies and feeling for what he liked to call his "John Thomas". Things, he told himself, were going splendidly.

Five minutes later things started to go even more splendidly when Carla, all flashing eyes and gleaming white teeth, put her hand in his other pocket and started to look for the same object. Colonel Wharton-Ware, who would be dead before morning, realised that this was the highpoint of his war – and damn Rommel.

At eleven o'clock, he staggered to his feet, flashing a glance down anxiously to see if his flies were buttoned up once more. They were. "So," he announced, slurring his words quite considerably, "ladies I think it is time I escorted you home. It'll be curfew soon and I don't want you charming damsels to get into any trouble with the naughty military policemen." He squeezed Yvonne's silken plump rump lovingly and said in a stage whisper, "It's I who is going to be naughty, what?"

The "damsels" giggled furiously.

The drunken Colonel took one last look at the belly dancer who was coming to the climax of her dance. Every inch of golden brown flesh seemed to vibrate; breasts and buttocks seemed threatened with destruction as she reached a final paroxysm. Head flung back looking gracefully drained, she sank into a chair next to an elderly general and asked in a husky voice, "Hello, darling. Have you a whisky for me?"'

"By George," the Colonel said at the sight. "Real hot stuff."

He felt his loins begin to tingle once more. Next moment he turned and followed the girls out to the waiting taxi.

They drove towards the Nile. Already the streets were beginning to thin out, though there were military policemen at every intersection. Traffic moved steadily over the Kasr El Nil bridge. Pinpoints of light, white, yellow and red, reflected in the viscous surface of the river.

He dismissed the taxi at the girls' houseboat from which they plied their trade. Their servant was waiting at the little pontoon bridge which led to the boat. "Achmed," Yvonne said.

"*Jewa. Ta'ala*, please madame." The servant held her hand delicately as she swayed across in her high heels.

Carla followed. In the yellow light of the lantern ahead, she gave a slight nod.

Achmed acknowledged it with a narrowing of his dark cruel eyes.

The Colonel followed, disdaining the proferred hand, and swaying dangerously as he crossed the little bridge.

Yvonne led the way down to the cabin below. There were silken cushions everywhere and a long low divan, coloured a dim red by the lamp. Yvonne reclined on the divan. Carelessly. To his delight the Colonel saw she wore no knickers and that she wasn't a true blonde after all.

Carla sat on the pile of cushions and clapped her hands. "Wine," she called.

Achmed called "*Jewa*". A moment later he came down bearing a silver tray with glasses and a bottle of white wine.

"Or would you prefer whisky, Colonel?" Yvonne said, stirring to pour the wine and revealing that delightful secret thatch once again.

"No thank you, my dear," Colonel Wharton-Ware answered. "Must try to keep a clear head for what is to come, what?"

Carla reached out and ran the backs of her fingers down

35

the side of his chubby, well-fed face. "Naughty boy." She feigned a yawn. "I think I'll take off this tight dress. It's hot and I'll be more comfortable."

Automatically the Colonel reached out for the glass, as Carla slithered out of the tight silk dress to reveal her shapely body clad in a sheer black silk petticoat, with nothing beneath it.

The Colonel gasped and downed the wine in one gulp. His blood raced. Carla had massive breasts. Now she reached inside the top of the petticoat and massaged her left breast suggestively. Then she took it out and proferred it to the gaping officer. "You like to kiss?" she asked in a husky voice. "Be my little boy."

"Oh yes, please," he gasped eagerly.

She tendered him the nipple. His mouth sank over it. He began to suck away, while she patted his balding pate, looking at Yvonne at the same time with a look of absolute boredom in her dark eyes.

Yvonne shook her blonde head as if in warning.

"Now, now, colonel darling," she chided him gently. "We mustn't be greedy – *yet*. We have all night to savour our pleasures. Take another glass of wine."

The Colonel reluctantly pulled his mouth away from Carla's swollen nipple. "Yes, yes, I suppose you're right, my dear." He accepted another glass of the sweet white wine and had another glimpse of that black thatch between Yvonne's spread legs as she leaned over to give him the wine.

He gulped down a hasty drink, feeling his face flush with the heat and lust.

Carla rose slowly from the cushions and this time she tendered her breast to the other whore. She looked over her shoulder as Yvonne slipped the nipple between her scarlet-painted lips and said, "You like exhibition, Colonel?"

Wharton-Ware's head whirled, "You mean," he gasped, "between the two . . . of you?"

Why naturally," she answered in that husky whisper of hers, gently putting her hand between Yvonne's legs. "You like watch what women do when they alone?" Softly she smoothed her long middle finger along the length of the thatch.

Yvonne shuddered violently, as if in the grip of an almost unbearable passion. Her head fell back and she moaned deep down inside her throat.

The Colonel downed the rest of his wine in one greedy gulp. He blinked his eyes rapidly. His vision was a little slurred. But he had to see this. In his time he had seen some things in the brothels of Bombay and the like. But never two white women performing together with such skill and passion. Now Yvonne had her legs spread as wide as she could get them, gasping frantically as Carla worked on her ever more fiercely, a brutish look on her hard face, as if she were more intent on giving pain than pleasure.

Frantically the Colonel reached for the bottle and took a swig right from the neck. He told himself it might clear his blurred vision. He *had* to see everything going on. He couldn't afford to waste a moment. Treats like this didn't come along every day.

But his eyes wouldn't clear. His head felt strange too. He shook it and suddenly to his great surprise he found himself on the floor looking up at the two whores who had ceased their "exhibition", as if by command. They wavered and swayed in his blurred vision. "What . . .

what happened?" he quavered in a voice he hardly recognised as his own.

Carla looked at him. Cruelly she said, "You got drunk, you fat pig."

"*Ssh*," Yvonne hissed and with a jerk of her head indicated the stairs which led to the deck above.

Vaguely Wharton-Ware heard the footsteps of someone descending the ladder. But he seemed unable to turn his head to see who it was.

A voice said something in Arabic which he couldn't understand. Heavy footsteps crossed to where the whores stood, what clothing they had on adjusted now.

Suddenly a large swarthy man with a bullet head and trim almost military moustache appeared. He had the build of a wrestler, which he had once been, and was big for an Egyptian, which he obviously was.

Weakly the Colonel tried to rise, but with a contemptuous jerk of his well-polished shoe, the big Egyptian pushed him back to the rug.

"I am going to ask you a question, Colonel Wharton-Ware," the Egyptian said in a deep commanding voice.

In a vague kind of a way, the Colonel felt a sense of alarm. How did this Egyptian know his name? He hadn't told the two tarts.

"I don't— "

"Be quiet," the Egyptian commanded in a voice used to giving orders – and having them obeyed. "What is so special about Major Hard's mission and what has the Royal Navy got to do with it?"

Wharton-Ware's sense of alarm grew. How did the Egyptian know this information? He had obviously seen Hard with the bearded naval officer, Christian, too. "I don't know what you're talking about," he said weakly.

38

"Look, you are in no position to lie to me," the big Egyptian snapped. "You are totally compromised. Drunk and with two whores."

Carla looked at Yvonne, but the latter shook her head. Gamel Nasser of the Egyptian Army was too dangerous a man to be rebuked about his use of the word "whore".

"In one minute," the Egyptian went on, "I shall have you stripped. Your photo will be taken in a compromising position with the two women – and I promise you it will be a very unsavoury photograph. A copy will be sent to your wife, your general and your regiment. Your reputation will be ruined."

"You wouldn't do that," Wharton-Ware said, a note of pleading in his voice now.

"I certainly would."

"But I know nothing really."

"What *do* you know then?" the big Egyptian persisted, dark eyes glittering, his big wrestler's hands clenched, as if he were very angry at something.

"All I know is that the general told me . . . the mission into Libya had been ordered by the PM."

"*PM*?"

"The Prime Minister," the Egyptian hissed. He looked thoughtful for a moment, while the Colonel stared up at him and the two solemn whores helplessly.

Then the Eygptian snapped something to Carla in Arabic. She looked very scared suddenly. Instinctively she clutched Yvonne's arm. Nasser looked at them contemptuously. Then he took out a wad of Egyptian pounds from his pocket and threw the notes carelessly on the divan. He gave the fat Englishman on the floor one last glance and then clambered back up onto the deck. The three of them could hear his heavy-footed passage across the pontoon bridge.

For what seemed an eternity, there was absolute silence inside the cabin, no sound at all save for the soft lap-lap of the water outside on the hull. Then Carla called, "Achmed," while Yvonne's painted face grew ever more worried.

Five minutes later the three of them threw Colonel Wharton-Ware's drugged, weighted body into the Nile . . .

SIX

The first day out was easy. The road was good. Occasionally the desert sand drifted across it and the vehicle convoy had to slow down for a while, but the two American Dodges which carried the patrol had four-wheel drive and they managed the sand easily. As the sun started to sink in the west, they reached a small Anglo-Egyptian military encampment. They did a couple of turns down and up the road so that everyone was aware that they were there, particularly the Egyptian soldiers. Then they filled up with petrol and still to make their presence very obvious brewed up and ate a meal of fried bully beef, followed by a rare luxury – tinned peaches. Then they rolled in their blankets and went to sleep.

Guardsman Smith, who had the midnight to one o'clock spell of sentry duty woke Hard precisely at one. He did the same with the others and then without the usual dawn "brew-up", they crept softly to the two Dodges. At Hard's command they began to push them clear of the camp. It was hard work but they managed it till they came to the descent 200 yards away. Here the two drivers jumped in, followed by the rest. The drivers thrust home first gear and took off their brakes. The Dodges started to roll. Hard flung a glance behind him. Nothing stirred in the little camp. They hadn't been spotted. By the instant the trucks began to gather momentum. The drivers turned on their engines. They came to life virtually noiselessly. A few minutes later they were speeding into the distance at a good 30mph.

By dawn the road was beginning to run out. On either side of the rough track, there rose great dunes of fine grained sand, so white and dazzling that they could have been snow. Above, the sky was a hard harsh blue with a sun that glowed like a yellow ball. "Won't be long, sir, before the fun and bleeding games start," Sergeant Williams, a tough little regular, who was a veteran of these long-range patrols, commented.

"Shouldn't be surprised, Sarge," Hard agreed, telling himself he hated the desert with its thirst and unrelenting heat, when he was in it but after a couple of weeks of the soft life back at base, he always longed for the wild freedom it offered him. He felt sure that the men experienced the same sensation. Back at base it was all bull and saluting – "if it moves salute it; if it don't, paint it white", as the old sweats cracked. Probably that's why most of them had volunteered for the LRDG in the first place. He cast a look in the rear-view mirror at their faces in the open truck with its twin machine guns mounted on the tripod. His men were bronzed, fit and terribly tough, their faces pared down to the very bone by the hardships they had undergone in the desert. Suddenly he felt very proud of them. They wouldn't let him down.

On the third day out, the little convoy by-passed at a safe distance, the occupied oasis of Ain Dulla on the eastern fringe of the Great Sand Sea. When they were safely away from the little oasis, an island of green in the middle of all that burning white, Hard allowed the team to brew up. While they filled an old petrol tin with sand and sloshed in petrol which would make the fire upon which to boil the tea water, Hard took a compass reading which would take them to the well-remembered "Easy Ascent".

An hour later they were tackling it. Guardsman Smith, their most skilled driver, had now taken over the wheel. He knew exactly what to do. He put his foot down hard on the accelerator. It was the only way not to get bogged down in the soft sand. The Dodge charged up the steep incline, rutted here and there by the tracks of previous vehicles of the LRDG. Then just as he reached the top, he swerved the wheel sharply to the right. The big Dodge slithered round in a wild whirling wake of white sand and halted there, shaking and quivering almost like a horse which had refused a jump. Down on the other side, the sand fell steeply. Hard flung a quick look at the other Dodge. It was making the ascent in good shape too. Little "Dicky" Bird who was driving knew his business well, too.

Smith wiped the sweat from his dripping brow with a brawny forearm. "I'll never get used to this bleeding Easy Ascent if I live to be a hundred which I won't, sir."

"You did very well, Smithie," Hard said. "All right, take her down."

Smith, his jaw taut, face set, slammed home first gear, and let out his clutch. Slowly, very slowly, twisting his wheel from side to side so that the truck went down the steep descent in a zig-zag pattern, he fought the Dodge to the bottom. Hard watched intently, saying nothing. He knew just how tricky this business was. One slight mistake and they'd be rolling down at a tremendous speed to crash at the bottom. Out of the corner of his eye, he saw that Dickie Bird was going down in the same manner, fighting every foot of the way. Twice the Dodge threatened to overturn and then both of them had done it and they were rolling forward at a steady 15mph. But now they started to bog down in the soft sand at least once an hour. Then everyone, including Hard, grabbed a shovel to begin the hard, back-breaking, time-consuming work of digging the wheels free to make channels so that they could place the steel mats beneath them and get the vehicles rolling again.

That afternoon, due to the delays, they made barely twenty miles. The heat was unbelievable. It beat down upon them relentlessly, keeping them lathered in sweat. The sand was murderous too, although they wore Arab headdress and goggles. It seemed to penetrate everywhere – ears, nose, mouth, body so that they scratched constantly as they laboured across that immense plain of sand, bare of anything, as if they were last men alive on the planet. That night after the usual brew up and a plate of corned-beef stew they fell into an instant exhausted sleep. Hard awoke about two. Now it was freezingly cold and he was glad of the warmth of his blanket. Above, the velvet sky was ablaze with the icy light of a myriad stars. For a few moments he realised just how insignificant they were. Puny little mortals going about their silly games of war, urged on by petty ambitions and promises. Then he forced himself to think of the task ahead.

In about another four days they'd be in the Tobruk area. By now the whole mass of Rommel's army would be in that same area, encircling the port and also the coastal road that led from Libya to Egypt. They would have to get across that road and through the German front line. They had done it before when they had attacked

German airfields and installations at places like Derna and Benghazi. But now the Germans would be alerted to their coming. He sucked his cracked lips. If only there could be some sort of a diversion long enough for them to slip through . . .

He was suddenly startled out of his reverie by a sound. It came from a long way off, but then sounds carried mile after mile in that trackless desert. There was someone else out there. But who? Or what?

He slipped out of his blanket. He shivered in the biting cold. Hurriedly he crossed over to the first Dodge where Sergeant Williams was doing his hour's "stag" or sentry duty. Noiselessly he slipped in beside him. He handed Williams a couple of boiled sweets. On sentry go they were not allowed to smoke. In the desert the glimmer of a cigarette end could be seen twenty miles off. Williams thanked him. All of them knew that sucking the sweets helped to pass the time. "Sarge," Hard asked, after Williams had popped one of the acid drops into his mouth, "did you hear anything just now?"

"No, sir, I can't say I did. Might it have been the wind? It was quite windy when I came on stag."

Hard shook his head. "No, it wasn't the wind. It's dropped altogether." He wound down the window and cocked his head to one side.

Williams did the same and both listened intently, their faces serious and coloured a silver hue by the icy light of the stars. Nothing. Finally Hard wound up his window again and said, "I could have sworn I heard something."

Williams did the same and said, "Well, none of our lads are out on patrol at the moment, sir. So, if there is somebody out there, well," he left the rest of his sentence unfinished.

45

"Yes," Hard agreed slowly and thoughtfully, "it can only be the enemy."

"Yer," Williams said, "bloody old Jerry . . ."

Next morning they set off again just after dawn when the air was still cool and fresh. Now the countryside began to change. The flat stretches of sand and those killing dunes gave way to broken, rugged country, made up of flat-topped hills, where the traction was good. Now their progress started to speed up and Hard could concentrate on his problems – navigation and the possible presence of the enemy – and leave the driving to the drivers.

Time and time again he scanned the blue rippling horizon, but it remained obstinately empty. If there had been anyone out last night, he told himself grimly, he's done a good job of vanishing.

At eleven, Hard ordered a halt. They would eat, have their "char" and rest a little before the real heat of the day commenced. At least when they were moving there was a slight cooling breeze. Stiffly the men clambered out of the Dodges. Dickie Bird was in charge of the brew this morning. He filled the square petrol tin with a shoveful of sand, poured some of their precious petrol into the sand. Then with a bayonet he stirred the mixture to the consistency of a batter and tossed a match into it. Whoosh, it went up in a burst of blue flame. Next minute the big blackened dixie was in place and the water was bubbling merrily while the men waited, chewing a little aimlessly on their hardtack biscuits.

Hard waited for a few minutes. Then he felt the first rumbles in base of his gut. Obviously he had caught the old "desert squitters". All of them did. It was due to the flies which were everywhere. "I'm going to take a spade for a walk lads," he announced, pulling the spade from

46

the side of the first of the Dodges and at the same time picking up a few leaves of "Army Form Blank", as they called lavatory paper.

The men responded with a faint burst of laughter and someone said, "If you ain't back in ten minutes, sir, we'll send a rescue party out looking for you."

Hard was used to the banter. Rank distinctions usually disappeared on this long-range patrols. Besides, he knew it was meant well; they all had been through the same. "And don't drink all the sodding char," he called over his shoulder, as he disappeared into the nearest wadi. He squatted just in time. He felt the twinge of pain in his lower gut and then got on with it. But even as he squatted engrossed in evacuating his bowels, he felt there was something wrong to his front. For a moment he couldn't pinpoint it. Then he had it. To the left, miles away but clearly visible, there was a glint of bright light. It winked off and on, as it moved along the ridgeline. "Christ," he whispered to himself.

His first instinct was to pull up his pants and hurry back to the others, but he resisted it. Instead he finished his business, pulled up his pants as if he had all the time in the world. Taking the spade, he proceeded to cover his faeces with sand and after that washed his hands with the same substance. Leisurely, spade over his shoulder, he clambered out of the wadi and strolled back to the others. He accepted his mug of "char" from Dickie Bird, who said winningly, "Sarnt-Major's char today, sir. Put a whole tin of evaporated milk in it. Yer could stand a spoon up in the dixie, it's that thick."

"Thanks," Hard said and savoured the rich brown liquid, apparently at ease, simply enjoying the taste. In

47

reality, his mind was racing, as he considered what he had just seen.

Finally he finished every last drop of the precious liquid. He scrubbed the mug out with sand and said, "Gather round. Make it look casual. Got something to say to you."

Sergeant Williams looked at him curiously. "Trouble at t'mill, sir?" he asked.

"Something like that. Now listen, lads," Hard went on. "While I was taking a crap out there in the wadi, I caught a glimpse of light being reflected from a moving object."

"Glass on car headlamps," Smith said promptly.

"Exactly. You know how we've always painted ours over so that they don't glint in the sun and give us away. All our patrols do." He gave a little shrug. "So all I can conclude is that the enemy is out there."

"Bit far out for old Jerry, sir?" Williams ventured. "Usually they stick pretty close to the coastal plain. They ain't got our knowhow in this kind of game."

"I know," Hard agreed. "Perhaps in the meantime they've developed long-range patrols. No matter. We've got to be prepared for trouble. I want you in half a mo' to check your weapons and the Brownings." He indicated the twin Browning machine guns on each truck. "Arm your grenades too. Usual drill if we're attacked on the move. Split up – makes us less of a target. Rendezvous once the trouble's over. Any questions?"

"Yessir." It was Tubby Henderson, the squad's supposed wit, a tubby Scot who managed to keep fat even on their short commons, "Will ye no transfer me to yon Pay Corps at the double, sir?"

Hard laughed softly, as did the others. The fat Scot was always good at defusing tense situations.

"All right, lads," Hard concluded, "let's get to it."

On the horizon the lights glinteed again and came to a stop.

SEVEN

"Hauptmann Graf von Almaszy zur Stelle, Herr General-feldmarschall," the middle-aged soldier reported in that soft Austrian dialect of his.

Rommel, his broad face lathered in sweat, looked up from his crude desk, made up of old ration boxes, and waved his whisk to drive away the flies which were everywhere. Before him stood the most unsoldierly officer he had seen in a long time. Tall and extremely skinny in long, drooping shorts, Count von Almaszy looked more as if he ought to be in an old people's home than in the *Wehrmacht*, so Rommel thought. "Ah, ah, the celebrated Count von Almaszy of the Brandenburgers.* Please be seated. You look as if you need a rest."

The Count bowed in the Viennese fashion and took the seat. "Thank you, Your Excellency. It is very kind of you. I have covered 200 kilometres on foot in the last four days and it is rather warm."

Rommel looked a little surprised. Not even the fittest of his young soldiers could do that. The old boy must be pretty tough. "Would you like something to drink?" he offered.

"An English whisky, if I may?" the Count ventured.

---

* Special German formation, equivalent to the SAS.

Rommel looked surprised. It was only nine in the morning. Still, he reasoned, the old boy needs it perhaps. *"Ordonanz,"* he bellowed, *"ein Whisky fur den Herrn Hauptmann."*

Heels clicked. *"Jawohl, Herr Feldmarschall,"* a voice shouted. A moment later a servant came in, gravely holding a tray with water, whisky and a glass on it.

He poured a stiff shot of whisky into a large glass and asked, *"Wasser, Herr Hauptmann?"*

Von Almaszy shook his grizzled head. "No thank you, water is too precious to waste."

Rommel's broad Swabian face cracked into a smile. The old boy wasn't only tough, he was a bit of a comedian too. *"Zum Wohle,"* he cried, dismissing the orderly with a wave of his fly swatter. The orderly put the tray on the desk and vanished.

Von Almaszy placed the glass level with the third button of his shirt, arm extended at a 45 degree angle, as army regulations prescribed, bowed to Rommel and then downed the fiery liquid in one gulp.

Rommel was impressed. In thirty years in the army he had seen some drinking in his time, but never an officer who could down a tumbled of whisky in one gulp at nine o'clock in the morning. *"Bravo, Herr Graf,"* he said in admiration. "I think that would have killed me."

"Good for the stomach in this climate, *Herr Feld-marschall,"* the old Count commented, his voice not even hoarse.

"Now then to business. What is the news from Cairo? What are the English intentions?" Rommel barked out the questions in eager anticipation. Once he had captured the great supply port of Tobruk, packed with months of supplies for the British Eighth Army, he would have the

51

means of advancing on the Egyptian capital. Once he reached Cairo and the Nile the war in the desert would be over – in Germany's favour.

"Cairo is in panic, my informants tell me," the Count replied, eyeing the captured bottle of Scotch greedily. "The English have evacuated most of their civilians. Their headquarters is burning secret documents. And the Egyptian Army is preparing to mutiny at any moment. Your Excellency."

"*Kapital . . . Grossartig!*" Rommel chortled, highly pleased at the information. "It is not only a matter of days. Finish off Tobruk and we march." He stared across the desert to where the Stukas were wheeling and diving over the beleagured port like metal hawks. Huge columns of black smoke, flecked at their base with angry cherry-red flames, rose into the harsh blue sky. "You see, their flak is hardly responding. The heart has gone out of them."

"They are South Africans," von Almaszy said. "Many of them, the Boers, hate the English. After all their fathers fought against the English. Their hearts are not in this battle for the British Empire."

Rommel beamed. "Exactly. All to the good. The sooner they surrender, the sooner I can get out and capture Cairo. Then I shall request a transfer to Europe. I am heartily sick of Africa."

Von Almaszy said nothing. Who would change the magic of Africa for the prosaic boredom of Europe? he asked himself. Aloud he said, "There is one thing *Exellenz*?"

Rommel looked at him hard. "What's that?" he rapped.

"I have intelligence that the English are sending out one of their long-range desert patrols. It's objective is probably Tobruk."

"So?" Rommel snorted. "What is that to me? They are simply a matter of pinpricks, a few aircraft destroyed here, a road blown up there." He shrugged expressively. "Annoying but of little significance to the outcome of the war."

"This one might be some more significance," von Almaszy said, eyeing the Scotch bottle hopefully.

"What?"

"I have learned from my contacts in the Egyptian Army that this mission was ordered by no other person than Winston Churchill."

Rommel sat up. "What did you say?" he barked.

The Count repeated his statement.

"*Donnerwetter*," Rommel cursed. "Now what would the leader of his country be doing ordering out an individual patrol. The Fuhrer in his infinite wisdom would never think of such a thing."

Patiently von Almaszy waited till Rommel was finished. He knew the Field Marshal was saying the words for effect. It was clear that Rommel was beginning to become worried. "We have our people waiting for this English patrol in the desert. I am sure they can stop them. What we need, of course, is a prisoner to tell us what they're up to."

Rommel's face brightened. "Of course," he agreed enthusiastically. "It is all very strange. We need to know what the English – a cunning race – are up to. But say your people in the desert don't stop the English – and after all the desert is a huge area – what then?"

It was a question that von Almaszy had been expecting and he was prepared for it. He smiled thinly and answered. "Then we have our people in Tobruk. They will tell us," he added simply.

Rommel beamed at him.

Von Almaszy looked pointedly at the bottle of whisky.

"Of course, of course," Rommel said hastily. "You shall have another drink. Why, look I'll pour it for you myself. You deserve it." And he did . . .

Two miles away Professor Challenger and Lisa ventured out of the big dugout for a breath of air. The bombing had stopped, but there was still some shelling, mainly directed at the perimeter. "I think it's safe enough for an hour or so," Professor Challenger had decided. "Must get some air." He had scratched his chin under the big beard, for both of them were now lousy with fleas, as all the defenders were, and added, "Might be able to take my shirt off and— " He had stopped and looked at Lisa. "Course you won't be able to do that."

His eyes had dropped to her delightful bosom and she had said, "I don't think it would do the troops' morale much good, if I did."

He had roared with laughter and had said, "On the contrary, I think it would do their morale a world of good."

Now the two of them walked slowly along the shattered front in the stifling heat, taking in the sights. Everywhere there was evidence of the tremendous punishment the port had taken in the last few days. The harbour was full of wrecks, their masts and funnels protruding above the surface of the oil-scummed water. Along the quayside, most of the white painted houses were minus their roofs, their walls pocked by shrapnel like the symptoms of some loathsome skin disease. Naturally there were soldiers everywhere. British ack-ack gunners in side hats, with half-smoked cigarette ends behind their right ears. South Africans, bronzed and beefy, wearing solar topees; and blacks from the labour companies, many of them in the shallows trying to salvage what they could from the wrecks under the command of white NCOs, many of whom carried pick-axe handles, waving them threateningly whenever the black labourers seemed to slacken off.

"What do you think, Professor?" she asked after a while, ignoring the stares of the soldiers, who looked at her, as if they had never seen a woman before. "How long will we be here?"

He looked down at her. He could see she was worried, not only by the danger she faced, he knew, but also by the threatening sexuality of the woman-starved soldiers. "Not long, I should think," he said reassuringly. "The authorities wouldn't want *us* to fall into German hands, not with what we know." He smiled down at her winningly.

She forced a brave smile herself.

To their right, a burly South African had waded into the water and was beating the naked back of one of the blacks, crying, in a thick Afrikaans accent, "Work, you lazy Kaffir dog! Work, or I'll knock the living shit out of you!"

The Professor shook his head. "One wonders," he said a little sadly.

She nodded her agreement. "Yes," she said. "It is not only in Germany where the Nazis are."

"But you must understand, Miss," a voice cut in from behind them, "that NCO has probably been brought up to believe that a black man is not much superior to a monkey. He doesn't regard him as a human being. He regards the blacks only as creatures who tend to his fields and clean his house."

They turned as one. A small neat man who wore glasses was standing there, smiling at them. He wore the badges of the South African Medical Corps and on his shoulders he had the two brass pips of a first lieutenant. The South African touched his hand to his solar toppee and added, "May I introduce myself? Lieutenant Smits of the South African Medical Corps." His name was obviously Boer, Challenger told himself, but the officer's accent was clearly English.

Challenger introduced himself and Lisa.

The little South African said, "Like yourselves, I needed a little fresh air. As soon as the shelling stopped I thought I'd leave my patients for a while and come up and get some."

"You're a doctor of medicine, I take it?" Challenger asked.

"Yes. Not a very good one," the little man said with a smile, "but I do my best to patch our poor chaps up when they get hit." He looked enquiringly at Lisa. "I don't suppose you're a doctor of medicine?" he asked. "We can always use some help, especially after all this shelling."

She shook her head. "No, I'm afraid not. My doctorate is in natural sciences, not medicine."

The little South African doctor smiled again. He seemed to smile a devil of a lot, Challenger thought. "I see. What a shame. I can detect you are not English either."

Challenger stepped in before Lisa could answer. Hastily he said, "Shall we get on with our walk before the shelling starts again?"

"Of course," Smits agreed with yet another thin smile. "Let's make the most of it before those damned

56

squareheads start bashing at us again." He shot Lisa a sharp look as he said the word "squarehead".

Challenger noted it, but could make nothing of it.

For a while they walked in silence, watching the half naked blacks salvaging what they could from the wrecked ships and a crowd of cheerful Tommies stripped to their underpants, trying to wash their clothes in the shallows. Out to sea, a black dot on the hard blue horizon, a plane droned back and forth and Challenger broke the heavy silence to ask, "One of ours?"

Smits, as ever smiling, shook his head. "I'm afraid not, Professor, one of *theirs*. It's one of their patrol aircraft. Always on the lookout to see that no one comes in or gets out of here. You see, Professor," he added and suddenly his smile had vanished, "none of us are ever going to get out of Tobruk now . . ."

EIGHT

"*I hate them!*" the young private hissed, as they crouched there in the sand. "I hate them with all my heart." His dark eyes rolled wildly. "I could kill all the English with my bare hands – all of them. Let them get out of our country and leave us in peace, the pigs." He spat drily into the sand.

"Be quiet," Lieutenant Amal hissed. He told himself that the soldier was like all the Delta people, hot-headed and hysterical, given to a lot of bold talk. But when it came to action, then they were not so eager.

He focused his glasses, taking care to shield the lenses so that the glint of glass did not betray his position. The sky was beginning to break up. Dusk was not far away. But from their positions on the ridge he could see the yellow Dodge grinding its way up the ascent quite clearly. He adjusted the lenses and counted the figures in the Dodge, outlined a stark black against the setting sun. There were six of them, and all of them seemed asleep save the driver, for their heads bumped back and forth every time the wheels of the Dodge hit an obstacle. He nodded his satisfaction, though he didn't like the look of those twin Brownings. Still, it was obvious the English suspected nothing. He turned and spoke to his platoon spread out behind the rocks. They were the best the

Egyptian Army and Major Nasser could find. Still, they were inclined to be hot-headed like the private lying next to him. "Remember," he lectured them in his educated Arabic, "the object is to capture one of them. We must find out what they are about. We shall fire. Kill some of them. Make the rest surrender. Is that clear?"

There was a rumble of assent from his men.

"Good," he continued, "now stand by your weapons – and no movement. We fire when the truck gets to that yellow rock. It is exactly 200 metres. I have measured it."

Obediently the men raised their old-fashioned Lee Enfields, British Army casts-off, but an exceedingly good rifle, Amal told himself. Behind the bren gun, his sergeant, his most trusted man, jerked back the bolt and tucked the butt into his skinny shoulder. They were ready.

Amal aimed his own rifle. It was a German Mauser bought on the Cairo black market. Some British soldier had brought it back from the desert fighting and had sold it there. It was the standard Afrika Korps weapon, but this one had telescopic sights. Probably it had been used by a sniper. He focused on the approaching truck. The men in it were as clear through the sight as they had been through his binoculars. He nodded his approval.

Now the Dodge was slowly approaching the yellow rock. Amal focused on the Englishman sleeping behind the Browning. He'd knock him off first. If the Englishman managed to start firing the twin machine guns, he knew his platoon would panic. They were the best, he knew, but there was no use fooling oneself about the fighting qualities of the Delta people. "Each man pick a separate target now," he ordered. "Aim for the widest part of the body, not the head."

The Dodge was almost there now. Amal started to take first pressure, curling a white-knuckled finger around his trigger. He had never been in action, but he felt no fear. Indeed he had a sensation of heady excitement. He sensed he was going to like what was soon to come. He felt no hatred of the English, as his soldiers did. Indeed, he quite liked the ones he had met in messes and bars. But he did detest the fact that they were occupying his country in that arrogant, lordly fashion of theirs. It would be good to see some of them, when taken prisoner, cringe.

The Dodge was parallel with the yellow rock. *"Now!"* he yelled. In that same instant he pressed his own trigger. The butt slammed into his shoulder. Behind the Brownings, the Englishman seemed to leap in his seat. Next moment he fell backwards and out of Amal's view.

All around him, his men were firing. Wildly, he thought. But they were hitting the target all right. He could see the clean silver of the Dodge's side where the slugs had struck home. Another of the English went down. Next to the driver, another slumped against the man at the wheel.

Frantically he pressed his foot down on the accelerator. Amal knew immediately what he was trying to do. He was attempting to reach the dead ground at the top of the incline, where he would be out of the way of their fire. "Get the driver!" he yelled urgently. "Come on, you dolts, hit the driver!" He raised his own rifle, ejected the spent cartridge and pumped the bolt back. He focused his sights on the Dodge's front right tyre. He controlled his breath and fired. He missed. Next moment, the driver of the Dodge, with its cargo of dead men, had disappeared into the dead ground.

For a moment, Amal did not act. What was he going to do? Then he woke to the danger of the driver escaping. They still needed that prisoner. "On your feet everybody," he yelled to his triumphant men, who were grinning like baboons and were slapping each other on the back, telling each other what great soldiers they were. "Come on – to the trucks. We can't let that driver get away. We need a prisoner."

Madly they rushed to the two Bedford trucks which had brought them this far, travelling through the German lines so that they could take the shortest route into the desert. Nasser had arranged it all with the Germans.

The drivers swung themselves in and started up, while the men scrambled into the back excitedly, knowing there was no danger. After all there were twenty of them to one Englishman.

In the dead ground, Dickie Bird grinned, despite the sweat pouring down his face. The trick had worked, though he told himself, he had nearly shat himself when the slugs had started coming so close. Now he pressed the Dodge's klaxon three times. It was the signal. He started to push the bodies out of the Dodge-sandbags covered with bits of the team's spare clothing. Then he waited for the fun and games to commence . . .

"Here they come," Hard said, as the first Bedford truck started to grind up the rock-littered descent. "Stand to everybody."

His men needed no urging. They had just spent a punishing three-quarters of an hour getting here on foot to establish the ambush. Now they wanted their revenge for the sweat-soaked effort.

Next to Hard, spread-eagled on the ground, Williams took aim with the ugly-looking piat, an anti-tank weapon, which had a powerful kick. A soldier needed all his strength to hold and fire it. All around him the others did the same with a variety of weapons.

The truck, trailing a wake of yellow sand behind it, was about 300 yards away now. Behind it a second one had appeared. It, too, was filled with men attired in the long robe of the Egyptian peasant. But Hard would have bet his bottom dollar at that moment that the men in the trucks were not civilians, but soldiers of the Egyptian Army.

"Let 'em get within range," he ordered quietly. "Don't want any of the treacherous sods to escape, do we now?"

There was a murmur of agreement among the men. Like all British troops, they hated the "Gippos", especially these traitors of of the supposedly allied Egyptian Army. As Williams always phrased it, "Rob yer frigging blind and then stab yer in the back, if they can sodding get away with it. That yer Gippo fer you."

Now the truck was less than 200 yards away and going at perhaps 10mph. A perfect target, Hard told himself. With the back of his hand, he wiped the sweat off his brow and cried, "*Open fire!*"

Next to him, Sergeant Williams pulled the trigger of his clumsy weapon. He grunted with pain as the padded butt slammed into his shoulder. The bottle-shaped projectile hurtled through the air as a volley of bullets sped towards the two trucks. Next moment the bomb exploded right on the bonnet of the first truck. It came to an abrupt stop. Thick white smoke started to pour from the ruptured engine. Next instant it exploded in a burst of fierce roaring flame.

Panic-stricken Egyptians tumbled from the damaged truck. They ran right into that concentrated fire. It wasn't war. It was a massacre. The Egyptians, caught completely by surprise in this ambush, hadn't a chance. They went down everywhere, screaming with pain throwing their arms around wildly.

Next to Hard, Sergeant Williams loaded rapidly. He fired again. Once more, the bottle-shaped rocket sped towards the second truck. Again Williams couldn't miss at that range. The bomb caught the truck in its rear axle. For one instant the truck reared in the air like a wild horse being put to the saddle for the first time. Then it crashed down. The axle shattered both wheels coming loose and trundling away like a child's hoop.

"All right, all right," Hard cried above the angry snap-and-crack of the small arms fire, "cease fire . . . don't waste any more ammunition on them. The Gippos have had it."

They certainly had. Those who were still on the feet dropped their weapons and raised their arms fearfully, their dark faces now coloured a greenish hue with fear. "Keep 'em covered," Hard ordered, rising to his feet, revolver in his hand.

"Ay," Williams agreed, "treacherous lot of buggers – Gippos. Watch 'em, lads." He rose, too, and unslinging his rifle, he followed Hard cautiously as he advanced on the handful of survivors, who were ignoring the moans and pleas of their wounded obviously intent solely on their survival.

"Where's the officer?" Hard demanded in Arabic, knowing now that they were Egyptian soldiers from the two Bedford trucks, which had been supplied to the Gippos by the British Army.

"I am he," a tall young man said in somewhat formal, but unaccented English.

Hard looked at the Egyptian officer, who was bleeding from a wound in his left cheek. "You can put your hands down. Tell your men to do the same . . . and tell them to look after the wounded. Can't leave the poor fellows like that."

The Egyptian looked at Hard defiantly but then he lowered his hands and gave instructions. Gratefully they lowered their hands and some of them bent to the wounded, but it was obvious they hadn't the first idea of how to treat the injured.

Hard clicked his tongue impatiently. "Sergeant Williams, see if they've got any field dressings and show 'em how to put them on, will you?"

Sergeant Williams shook his head, as if it was beyond belief that anyone should want to help a Gippo. Still, he obeyed the order, as Hard turned back to the young man, who still stared at him defiantly, dark eyes full of hatred. "Now then what's all this about?" he demanded. "Who sent you here, eh?"

"You waste your breath. I will not speak."

"You know I can have you shot for this. It's plain treachery."

The Egyptian laughed contemptuously. "Then have me shot. There are hundreds, thousands of patriots, to take my place. Do you think you can stop a whole nation by killing me, or hundreds like me? Soon British rule in Egypt – indeed, all over the Middle East – is almost finished."

"*Be Silent*! I'm no damned politico," Hard snapped, losing his temper a little, "I'm a soldier. Now then tell me what I want to know. This is your last chance. You deserve to die and you will, if you don't speak."

64

The Egyptian wavered for a moment, then his handsome young face, with the trickle of blood congealing on it, hardened again. "Do what you will," he said in that stilted English of his. "Speak I will not."

Hard admired the young man's bravery, but he knew he had to do it. Without the officer the other Egyptians would be totally lost. Their food and water would last them a few days and then they would die because they wouldn't be able to find their way out of the desert. He had to be killed. Wasn't he a traitor? Besides he had told him, indirectly, all he needed to know. The Egyptians were working for the Germans. That meant the Germans knew about the patrol. He guessed they didn't know its purpose – the rescue of the two civilians. But he had to assume that the enemy knew that the patrol was heading for Tobruk. So the Egyptians *had* to die before they had chance to report the present position of the patrol.

Mind made up, Hard swung round on Guardsman Smith. "Check those trucks, will you, Smithie? If there's a radio in them, destroy it."

"Sir," Smith actually stamped his right foot down as if he were on parade back at Pirbright Barracks.

Hard gave a half-smile and added, "All right, the rest of you, break the firing pins of all the Gippo weapons. We don't want 'em shooting us in the back as we move off." He indicated the two Dodges which were now nosing their way over the escarpment towards them. "Sergeant Williams."

"Sir?" Williams answered.

Hard nodded his head in the direction of the young officer, "Get rid of him," he said without emotion.

"Sir," Williams answered, equally without emotion.

For a moment the young officer panicked. Then,

hastily, he pulled himself together. "We shall bury you yet, you English."

"Come along now then," Williams said not unkindly. He took hold of the Egyptian's arm. Without resistance he let himself be led away. They disappeared round the bend, watched by the prisoners and their captors in a heavy silence.

There was a single shot, Moments later Sergeant Williams came back, rifle slung over his shoulder. He kept his gaze fixed on the ground. The Egyptians started to sob.

Hard tugged at the end of his nose, as if embarrassed. He wasn't. He knew he had made a fateful decision. When the Egyptian soldiers failed to return, their masters, German and Egyptian, would reason that the British had killed them. Now if they were captured, there would be no merry for them. They would be shot out of hand, too.

He turned and called, "All right, we've spent time enough here." He looked at the wailing Egyptians, knowing that soon they would be dead too. "Mount up, lads."

Five minutes later they were rolling once more, the men silent, each man wrapped in a cocoon of his own thoughts and apprehensions. No one looked back . . .

Book Two

The "Mucky Duck" Goes to War

"Seems to me, sir . . . the squareheads'll be clustering around like frigging bees round the frigging honey pot."

CPO Thirsk to Lt Christian, June 1942

ONE

The explosion shook more stone chips from the roof of the cave. Sitting in the tin bath with the girl washing his back, Lt Christian barked, "Can't even get a sodding bath in peace!"

Cara, as she called herself, smiled at him, as if he were a spoiled child, though with his beard, breath reeking of whisky and those fierce blue eyes, he would have made a most unlikely baby.

Since he had been based at Malta, Christian had been living with the girl for some six months. Together they inhabited one of the island's caves, not too far from the docks. Hence they were always being bombed. But the roof was tremendously thick and Christian reasoned that it would withstand anything but a direct hit. Though Christian wasn't given much to expressing affection, he liked Cara well enough in his own rough and ready fashion. She cooked their meagre rations, washed his clothes and, when he was sober enough, she gave him pleasure in bed.

He looked up at her now, as she wrung out the sponge and prepared to wash his front. He guessed she was about twenty, a slight, dark girl with dark flashing eyes and a merry face when she wasn't worrying about her family somewhere in the interior. Of course, strict Catholics that they were like most of the islanders, they had cut her off once she had gone to live with Christian. All the same she trudged out to them through the air raids every couple of days or so to take them whatever they could spare from their own meagre rations.

She started to wash his chest and then lower down. He liked the feel, but he didn't tell her that. He'd learned in his long life and experiences with women of all countries and colours, never to spoil a woman. "Get an uppity woman, shipmates," he was wont to proclaim in some pub or other, "and you have a tyrant. Keep 'em in their place and they're all right," and with that off his chest, he would take another drink, a look of righteous self-assurance on his fierce, bearded face.

"You sail this day, Christian?" she asked, rubbing the sponge skilfully and pleasantly around his testicles.

"No, not today, Cara," he reassured her. "Just a bit of make do and mend, I'd think. I'm waiting for a signal, you see. Hey, none o' that," he snapped, but without anger.

She had pulled his penis and grinned. Obviously she was happy he wasn't sailing yet. The Germans and their Italian allies were always on the lookout for ships leaving Malta. "All right," she commanded, the merry look on her face for once. "You finished. Stand up. I dry."

Obediently he stood up. She took the rough old Navy towel and began to pat him dry, as if he were a delicate baby. He didn't mind. In fact, Christian quite enjoyed it. Despite the ever present danger of being killed in the beleagured island, Christian thought that these last few months in the cave with Cara had been some of the happiest in his life.

She finished drying him and dropping the towel, leaving him standing naked on the square piece of

70

carpet, which he had "borrowed" from somewhere or other. She went to the rough wooden table and asked, "The plaster now?"

"Yes, put the ruddy thing on. In the old days back in Hull, my chemist in Hedon Road used to say the old Wintergreen would burn the bollocks off a bull."

She only half understood his words, but as she advanced on him with the plaster, trying to get her forefinger between it and the paper to which it was attached, she asked, "Why you wear? It is very hot."

"Has to be to be any good, yer daft ha'porth," he snorted, but without rancour. "Why do I wear it? I'll tell yer why. Because I've got a bloody rheumaticky shoulder. I don't want it to seize up. Then their Lordships would beach me for good. And I'm not ready for that yet." He gasped suddenly as she slapped the Wintergreen plaster against his right shoulder. He broke out into a sweat immediately. "By gum," he exclaimed, "that's doing it a world of good already."

She smoothed the plaster till all the wrinkles had vanished. "Right, Christian, now you dress."

For once he returned her grin and quipped, "Oh, I thought you'd put me trousers on for me."

She made as if she were going to grab his testicles and he said hurriedly, "All right, all right, I'll do it myself."

Five minutes later he was dressed in his battered uniform. He patted his hip pocket to reassure himself that his precious flask of whisky was there, then he said, "All right, what are yer waiting for? I'll have to be off. Give us a kiss."

She flew to his arms. He embraced her warmly as she pressed a wet kiss to his mouth and attempted to slide her tongue between his lips. He pushed her away from

71

him and slapped her rump. "Now none of that there here. At this time of the morning. You ought to be ashamed of yourself, my girl."

With that he was gone out into the blinding sunshine of yet another day of war on Malta. The dusty road between the ruins leading towards the Grand Harbour was packed with sailors, some in dungarees, white caps tilted to the back of their heads, Woodbines stuck behind their ears. They would be for the working parties. Others were in full rig. Obviously they'd be setting sail this fine morning. Automatically, Christian looked upwards at the clear blue sky. A black dot droned steadily round and round. "Bloody squarehead," Christian snorted to himself. It was the German reconnaissance plane, which always appeared over the Grand Harbour area at this time of the morning, which the ack ack gunners had given up trying to knock out of the sky because the German was beyond their range. Now the plane's radioman would be busy signalling back to the German fields in Sicily the latest details of all the shipping in the harbour.

"*BOMB ROME!*" the sign painted on the side of a bombed house proclaimed.

"Ay, bomb the bloody lot of 'em," Christian muttered his agreement under his breath, "let the ruddy Pope have a taste of what we're getting here."

He stopped to let a party of ratings march past, lugging great white kitbags on their backs. The chief petty officer in charge was an old hand. He caught a gimpse of Christian out of the corner of his eye and barked, "All right then, swing them arms. Bags o'swank. Open them legs – nothing will fall out. If it does, I'll pick 'em up for you. Remember you're the new rich, with one bob a day hard living allowance. Not like them poor dockers on a tenner a week and what they can nick. *Eyes right!*" The sticky CPO swung Christian a tremendous salute. Christian winked. He knew the type of old. The CPO winked back.

He let the harassed matelots pass, then he walked over to the entrance to the flag office. Here he showed his pass to the armed sentries in their sandbagged enclosures and went inside.

He was shown into the flag officer's office almost immediately. He saluted the flag officer, a big bluff captain in whites, rows of ribbons on his burly chest. "Ah it's you, Christian. Sit down. Take the weight off your feet."

"Thank you, sir." He sat down.

The flag officer shoved a silver cigarette box towards over the big paper-littered desk, "Smoke if you wish."

"Don't touch them, sir, thank you. Try to keep my habits clean."

The captain looked at Christian's red-rimmed eyes and said, "Pull the other, Christian, it's got bells on it. We'll all drink on Malta. It's about the only thing we've got plenty of – booze." He smiled and then he was businesslike. "I know from the signals from their Lordships in London that you are to undertake a very important secret mission."

Christian's eyes lit up. "Has the signal to get up steam come through, sir?" he asked eagerly.

"Not exactly," the captain answered.

"Oh," Christian said, feeling a little disappointed.

"Now, look here, we're running a convoy into Malta this night. Of course, the Huns have already spotted it. They always do at Gib, thanks to those damned dagos in Spain who spy for them. Anyway so far the convoy has been pretty lucky. Only one merchantman sunk and a destroyer escort damaged." He let his words sink and looked at Christian's tough bearded face as if he were searching for something hidden there.

Christian nodded his understanding, wondering what all this had to do with him. The captain soon enlightened him.

"Now as you know the Huns have got over 300 aircraft on Sicily by now and unlike the Eyeties they press home their attacks. They're trying to starve us into surrender by bombing our supply convoys and we are pretty sure they'll make an allout effort to have a go at this one while it's still in harbour. Tonight the whole defence system is going to be placed on maximum alert to meet the expected attack. Now Christian I have been signalled by their Lordships that your vessel, the *Black Swan*," he gave a fleeting smile as if he knew, too, the usual name given to the *Black Swan*, "must not be damaged at any cost. So one hour before the convoy approaches the Grand Harbour, Christian, you are to sail for Gibraltar, you'll be safer there. Can you get up steam etc. in time?"

Christian nodded and said, "Of course, sir. She might be a bit of an old tub, the *Black Swan*, but she's in good mechanical shape."

"Good," the captain sounded relieved. Obviously the Lordships in London were breathing down his neck. He rose. It was the signal that the meeting was over.

Christian rose too and put on his cap so that he could salute.

The captain stretched out his hand. "The best of luck to you, Christian, whatever your job is."

"Thank you, sir." He saluted and went out.

There were sailors, civilian dockers, ack-ack gunners everywhere. The noise was tremendous: the crash of steel hawsers, the insane, nerve-racking chatter of the riveters' guns as the men prepared for the entry of another precious convoy and cleared the wreckage of the previous night's raid.

Christian pushed his way through the throng, clambering over chunks of still-smoking masonry, cursing when anyone obstructed him for he was now a man in a hurry. He turned a bend in the quay and there she was – the "Mucky Duck".

Every time he saw his "command", Christian was shocked anew at her appearance. Specked with rust and unpainted these many months, the tall single smokestack's camouflage paint peeling, the *Black Swan* looked as if she were some hulk salvaged from the bottom of the ocean. All that was lacking was dripping seaweed and barnacles attached to her hull.

But she's a tough old bitch, he told himself, as he crossed to the ship, stinking of fuel, oil and rust. She had weathered many a storm, all 600 tons of her. With her 1200 HP triple expansion engine, she was using the same kind of power that could move a 5000 ton freighter.

Old CPO Thirsk was waiting for him on the littered deck. He swung the skipper a tremendous salute and tried at the same time to get a whiff of his breath. As he told his fellow petty officers when they were off duty, "When the Old Man's got a skinful, he's a real bastard. But when he's just had five or six, he's bearable."

"Morning, sir," Thirsk said, "what's the drill?"

Christian looked from left to right. It was known that the Italians had spies among the Maltese. "Keep it under your hat, but we're sailing at midnight before a convoy comes in. Just work the ship up nice and casual like. We've got all the stores and ammo we need for where

75

we're going, which I won't tell you at this moment. I'm off to my cabin."

"Ay, ay, sir," Thirsk barked and swung him another tremendous salute. Despite the "Mucky Duck's" appearance, CPO Thirsk, with his lined face and grey hair, was a stickler for naval discipline. Behind his back, the crew said he'd been in the Royal Navy so long that he had served with Nelson. Naturally he denied it, but sometimes when he had had a drop of "Nelson's Blood," he wondered if it might not be true; he seemed to have been in the Navy for ever.

Christian entered the "cabin" a steel box that contained a bunk, a table and a battered leather chair, that stank of rust and stale tobacco. Briefly he glanced through the papers and signals that "Sparks", their wireless operator, had placed on his table. Then he had a quick look at the chart, though he knew this part of the "Med" like the back of his hand. Then he thought he might have his first drink of the day. After all it was already 8.30 in the morning. It was then, just as he took the first slug from his battered silver flask, that it struck him: how was he going to tell Cara?

TWO

It was dark now. Malta was totally blacked out. Indeed by now most of the population and the garrison would be underground, waiting for the airraids to start. Already searchlights were parting the inky darkness above the island with their icy white fingers. It had grown cold and Christian buried his head deeper into the collar of his blue duffle coat, feeling the seawind on his bearded face. Down on the deck one of the ratings, still in his shirt sleeves, was doing some job or other, singing over and over again in a monotonous refrain, *"I've got spurs that jingle, jingle, jingle . . . as I go riding merrily along.'*

Christian shook his head in wonder. He was another "hostilities only" man, men who would serve only in wartime, but like the rest of the crew who were the same, he had obviously taken to the sea like a duck to water.

They were leaving the entrance to the Grand Harbour and Christian turned to CPO Thirsk who was at the wheel. "Full ahead, Chiefie. We want to be out of here before that poor bloody convoy docks. They're going to take some stick this night."

"Ay ay, sir," Thirsk growled in his thick East Coast accent and repeated the order down the tube. The "Mucky Duck's" engines started to throb ever louder and Christian could feel the deck vibrate beneath his feet. He nodded his approval. The old tub didn't look much cop, he told himself, but she had plenty of muscle. They started to draw away quickly.

For a moment or two, Christian allowed himself to dwell on the evening two hours before. As he had anticipated, Cara had taken the news that he would sail that night badly. First she had cried, then she had grown angry. "Why you do this?" she had exclaimed, eyes flashing, hands held out dramatically. "You too old. Why you do?" Then she had become passionate. "You make love to me. Come fuck . . . fuck . . . quick!" and she had begun to claw at his flies, as if she couldn't get at him quick enough. She had been on top of him when she had suddenly broken down and had fallen on his naked chest weeping broken-heartedly like a grief-stricken child.

He was a hard man, but his heart had gone out to her. He had forgotten his own pleasure and had clasped her in his brawny arms tenderly, stroking her hair, trying to soothe her.

After a while she had stopped crying and in the harsh white light of the hissing petroleum lantern she had looked at him and had said quite baldly, as if it were a matter of known fact, "They kill you, I know. They kill you, Christian."

"Of course, they won't," he had answered. "The squareheads have tried to kill me in two wars and I'm still here yet."

She had shaken her head firmly, her raven black hair falling over her thin, tear-stained face. "Yes, they will," she had said defiantly.

She had hardly looked at him, as he had prepared to leave. He had given her the last of his money, four shillings short of a fiver. It wasn't much, he had realised and as afterthought, he had unstrapped his silver watch, which she would be able to pawn if she needed more money – there were plenty of pawnshops around the harbour. "Worth another ten quid, I should imagine," he had said, handing it to her.

She had known the value of the watch to him and had turned it over to read the inscription on the back, saying the words slowly and with difficulty, "For Lt. Commander B. B. Christian . . . from the crew of H . . . M . . . S. . . . *Orion* . . . June 1940."

The crew had given him it just after he had won his DSO at Dunkirk. He had gone on a blinder in London and had, in his drunken rage, punched some Admiralty flunkey, heavy with gold braid, in the nose. Now he couldn't even remember why. But it had cost him one rank and the command of the destroyer, *Orion*.

She had looked up from the watch to where he had stood, knotting on his tie. "Now I know you not come back." Then she had gone to the one chair, turned it round and had sat stubbornly facing the wall. She hadn't even responded when he had said goodbye . . .

Christian sighed. Life was bloody hard, he told himself. But she'd be all right, he consoled himself. She was young and pretty. There'd always be other malelots, if anything—

"Sir," CPO Thirsk's voice cut into his reverie.

"What is it, Chiefie?"

"Over there to starboard . . . Can you see, sir?"

Christian peered through the darkness. Then he saw it – a dull red glow on the horizon, flickering on and off. It was the kind of glow he had seen far too many times in this war. He knew what it was immediately. "The convoy," he snapped. "Somebody's bought it, poor sod."

"Looks like it to me, sir," Thirsk agreed grimly. "And with that fire raging, the squareheads'll be clustering around like frigging bees round the frigging honey-pot."

"Yes, I don't think yer far wrong there, Chiefie." Christian said slowly. "Christ, what a bloody mess and we're hardly out of bloody Malta."

The old petty officer knew what the skipper meant. The burning ship had placed him in a quandary. All convoys to Malta had orders not to stop for any vessel which had been hit or dropped behind due to engine trouble. Their first duty, the commodores in charge of the convoys knew, was to get the supplies through to the hard-pressed island. The laggards would have to look after themselves. But the "Mucky Duck" wasn't part of a convoy. Christian could, within reason, do what he liked. He could attempt to rescue any survivors or he could just sail on to Gibraltar.

Christian cursed again. "All right, Chiefie," he said in the end, as if he were angry with himself, "we can't let the poor buggers drown. Set a course for her." He kicked the bulkhead in his irritation.

Half an hour later the carrier loomed up out of the darkness, an enormous floating platform listing badly to port, the fire crews busy putting out the remaining fire on her deck with their hoses.

"Hope they get that sod out by the time they reach Malta," Thirsk grunted, as they sailed on, heading for the glow which was now growing ever clearer, so that occasionally they could see the the stark outline of the blazing ship, which Christian guessed was probably a large freighter. Already he was wondering if the "Mucky Duck" might not be able to tow her to Gibraltar.

With the ship clearly outlined on the horizon now,

flames searing her deck like a gigantic blowtorch, they started to run into the first survivors. There were about half a dozen of them shocked, faces black with oil, as they looked up at those of the ratings on the tug, crying for help. Hastily Christian had the nets put over the side and in minutes they were being hauled up and taken to the galley, where the cook, "Dirty Dick", was busy lacing scalding hot tea with rum for them. *"Torpedoed . . . torpedoed,"* they kept saying over and over again, as they sipped the tea, as if it were some kind of litany, *"torpedoed"*.

Now, though he knew it was dangerous to do, Christian ordered the "Mucky Duck" to stop while he and Thirsk went over in the power dinghy to the blazing freighter. She was still high in the water despite the huge jagged gash in her bows where the torpedo had struck and which had caused the skipper to order "abandon ship". With luck they might be able to douse the flames taking her in tow.

Hastily he and Thirsk clattered up the iron-runged ladder, which was pretty hot to the touch. A man in an officer's cap stared down at them, his features hollowed out to red death's head by the lurid light of the fire. In his right hand he clutched a bottle. *"Welkom,"* he said, "Vil you have a drink with me, *Engelsman?"*

"Pissed as a newt," Thirsk said behind Christian.

Christian hauled himself over the railing and said hurriedly, eyeing the blazing rigging and the mast which would obviously come down in a minute, "Christian of the Royal Navy's tug HMS *Black Swan*. Can I be of any assistance to you?"

The fat middle-aged Dutchman shook his head. "No use," he said with an air of finality. He took a large drink of the Genever the bottle contained.

"You mind if I take a look?" Christian persisted. He always hated to lose a ship.

"*Nein*. You look." the Dutch skipper waved his arm expansively and said, "*Kom*."

Together, shielding their faces against the heat of the fire, they clambered over the wreckage and peered down the companionway. Obscene belches were coming from below, indicating to Christian that giant air bubbles were exiting through the wrecked hold. They went down the iron steps. The companionway was knee-deep in water. A confused mess of loaves of bread, tins, potatoes floated back and forth. With it, suspended by his rubber lifebelt, was the cook, not a blemish on him, save that he was minus his head. "Good cook," the Dutch skipper commented, as they worked their way round the dead man. "Best I know in forty years at sea." He touched his fingers to his lips like a connoisseur, "What dumplings with liver he makes."

Thirsk shook his head. They waded a little further. The ship's cat lay curled on a crate which wafted back and forth in the water. It looked as if it were asleep, but its paws were soaked in blood. It was dead. Just as the two ratings were who had been slammed against the metal wall by the impact of the torpedo with such force that they stuck there like grotesque human sculpture. "Lord, bless us and save us," Thirsk gulped.

Suddenly the freighter gave a great lurch. From some-where there came an angry hiss of a lot of steam escaping. Christian knew what that meant. The boiler room had just flooded. "Come on," he said, "let's get out of here. There's no chance of saving her now." They started to lark their way back to the deck. The skipper took one final swig of his gin and tossed the empty bottle into the water next to the dead cook. "What dumplings with liver," he said sadly.

Outside on the deck, the flames were reaching ever higher and, above noise of escaping steam and the eruptions of the giant air bubbles, Christian thought he could hear the distant drone of an aircraft engine. "Come on, skipper. Over the side with you. There's no time to be lost now."

The fat Dutchman suddenly looked stubborn. He shook his head and said, *"Nein.* I do not go."

"Why not?" Christian snapped. "There's nothing you can do now here."

"I have three ships torpedoed under me since 1940," the Dutchman said obstinately. "Why go on? I go down with the old pot."

"Don't be a damn fool," Christian said urgently. The sound of aircraft engines was getting closer.

The Dutchman crossed his arms across his fat chest. "No, I have said all."

Christian wasted no more time. He nodded to Thirsk who was standing behind the Dutchman. He knew what to do. He pulled the piece of lead piping which he always carried (after a lifetime of service in foreign ports he had learned always to be careful) out of the special pocket inside the leg of his trousers and slapped it down on the Dutchman's bare skull. He went out like a light. Minutes later the two of them were manhandling him down to the dinghy as the first of the enemy flares started to come down, turning night into day.

THREE

The Junkers found them at dawn. Just as the sky started to tinge a blood-red, with the sun hanging over the lip of the horizon, as if reluctant to rise any further, three of them came in from the north.

On the bridge Thirsk pressed his button. The klaxons sounded their urgent warning. The off-duty men tumbled out of their bunks. Immediately there was hectic activity, as men doubled for their duty posts, putting on their helmets, while the gunners swung their weapons round to meet the challenge.

Next to Thirsk, Christian flung up his glasses. The Junkers 88 bombers slid into the bright calibrated lenses of the binoculars. They were still flying in formation. In a moment, he knew, they would break up for individual attacks. The question was – from what direction?

"Are they carrying torpedoes?" Thirsk at the wheel asked urgently.

"No," Christian rasped.

"Thank God for that," Thirsk said. Christian knew why. They had a better chance of dodging bombs. Torpedoes would have been another matter.

"Here they come!" he yelled. "They're breaking up *now!*"

Down below the gunners swung their "Chicago pianos"

84

– massed banks of heavy machine guns – round. They tensed, following every movement of the two-engined bombers.

Now the first Junkers was coming. The plane seemed to skim the water, churning it up into a wild fury with its prop wash. Christian clenched his fists with suppressed tension, as he waited for the battle to commence. The Junkers was coming in fast. He knew the tactic. Just before it reached the "Mucky Duck", it would rise a couple of hundred feet to drop its bombs. It had to so that it didn't blow itself up. It would then be that the "Mucky Duck"'s gunners would have the one real chance to knock the bastard out of the sky.

Now Christian could see every detail of the bomber, the camouflaged fuselage, the sky-blue belly, the black and white Maltese cross on its side, even the dark-outlined figure of the pilot behind the glistening perspex canopy.

"The bastard's climbing!" Thirsk yelled excitedly.

Christian flashed a look at the nearest gunner. He had swung his "Chicago piano" round. He was going to fire. "*Now*," he yelled, though he knew the man wouldn't be able to hear him. Suddenly the roar of the Junkers' twin engines filled the whole world. But before the gunner could fire, Sparks manning the "Holman Projector" did. The Holman was the joke of the Fleet. It used steam from the engine room to fire a grenade into the sky. Most times crews used it to fire hot potatoes from one ship to another. Now Sparks used it in earnest.

Mouth gaping, Christian watched as the dark ball of the grenade, spinning round and round, raced upwards towards the enemy plane. Down below the gunner opened fire. Tracer sped to meet the Junkers like glowing golf balls. But the grenade beat the bullets. In an angry flash of yellow-red flame it exploded just underneath the Junkers' port engine. Like a great metal leaf, the wing, severed from the fuselage, started to tumble to the sea. Frantically the pilot, clearly visible in his glittering canopy, fought to control the plane. In vain. It fell out of the air. Next instant it had plunged into the sea, bursting through the surface and plunging straight to the bottom. No one got out.

A ragged cheer went up from the crew of the "Mucky Duck" and Thirsk grunted, "One down and two to go— " The rest of his words were drowned by the whistle of bombs. The second bomber coming in from starboard was dropping its bombs.

"Hard to port!" Christian yelled instinctively, as the bombs came raining down.

Thirsk reacted with surprising speed for such an old man. He wrenched the wheel round. The "Mucky Duck" reeled alarmingly. Just 50 feet away or so, the bombs struck the water. Huge gouts of whirling, wild water erupted upwards. Shrapnel hissed through the tug's shrouds lethally. A radio mast went. It tumbled to the deck in a flurry of angry blue sparks. A crewman yelled in pain and stared puzzled, or so it seemed, at his right arm from which blood jetted in a bright scarlet stream.

Then the bomber was soaring into the sky followed by a stream of angry tracer. The Junkers had evidently dropped its bomb load and was heading back to its base in Sicily. But there was still the third one, and Christian had an uneasy feeling that its pilot was going to press home his attack with all his might.

Bravely the German pilot skimmed above the water, the tracer criss-crossing in a white fury in his path. Christian could see him quite clearly. He knew that it took a lot of courage on the German's part to press home his attack at this height. But he knew, too, that the German was determined to blow the "Mucky Duck" out of the water to avenge the deaths of his comrades.

At the wheel, CPO Thirsk tensed. He was trying to outguess the German. At the moment he was zig-zagging at regular intervals. In a moment, when the attack was imminent, he'd change the pattern radically. But when?

Now the Junkers was only 200 yards away. It started to make height. It was preparing for the bombing run. On the deck, the gunners blazed away, aiming at the bomber's pale-blue belly. Metal flew from the Junkers like steel rain. But still it kept on. *"Here it comes!"* Thirsk yelled and wrenched the wheel round.

The "Mucky Duck" shuddered at every plate. She heeled violently and Christian grabbed a stanchion to prevent himself from falling over.

The next moment the bombs came raining down. Eyes bulging from his head like those of a man demented. Christian watched in awe as the stick came ever closer. One huge eruption of violent water after the other. The plane flashed over the tug like a giant metal hawk, dragging its evil black shadow behind it.

Later Christian always maintained that he had seen the bomb coming. *"Hit the deck,"* he cried as he did so, knowing that no one could hear him, but it was an instinctive reaction.

As Thirsk twisted the wheel desperately to get out of the bomb's path, Christian tensed. He had a momentary glimpse of a blinding white light. It changed next instant to a vivid cherry red. Then the deck came up to meet him, as the "Mucky Duck" shuddered crazily. The blast lifted the rim of his helmet and knocked it backwards. He felt an excruciating pain in his ears and for a moment thought that his ear-drums had gone. *"Don't let go,"* he commanded himself, as the "Mucky Duck" lurched badly to one side. *"Come on, Christian, keep in frigging control, will you."* He felt his knees begin to go. Madly he clutched the stanchion, holding on like a boxer refusing to go down for the count of ten. Then the plane was gone and he felt a sudden sensation of calm, as the firing died away and all was silent, save the wounded chug-chug of the "Mucky Duck's" engine . . .

"It's a bit of a shambles, sir," Thirsk said and sniffed, as if he had just smelled something unpleasant.

"You can bloody well say that again," Christian said and stared around at the mess of twisted metal and debris which littered the ship's interior. The bomb had gone through the upper deck exploded and wrenched a great jagged hole in the bow just above the water line. But already the "Mucky Duck" was beginning to take water and the two of them were already up to their knees in it. "What's the pump like? On the blink?" He indicated the 8-inch pump which was powered by petrol.

"No sir," Thirsk said. "Looks all shipshape and Bristol-fashion to me."

"Thank God for that. Then we'd better get cracking with the patch before we ship any more water than we have. Stop engines."

"We're going to be a sitting duck if we stop engines now, sir!" Thirsk objected, a worried look on his lined old face.

"We're a sitting duck as it is," Christian said grimly. "The squareheads or the Eyties can come along and pick us off just any time they want. Come on, let's get cracking."

"Ay ay, sir," Thirsk said without too much enthusiasm.

He knew exactly what making a patch for the damaged hull entailed – a lot of bloody hard work.

Five minutes later the "Mucky Duck" had heaved to. Those not engaged in making the patch now stood watch. Every gun was manned and those on watch carried rifles. They wouldn't be much good against enemy aircraft, but it made the lookouts feel they were capable of doing something, as they scanned every quarter of the bright blue June sky.

Now as the 8-inch pump chugged away, trying to drain the water out of the hold, the gang with their shoes off and trousers rolled up to their knees, as if they were kids going paddling, started fixing wooden planks across the gaping hole, plank by plank. Each one seemed to take an eternity to fix with its "walking sticks", lengths of iron rod, threaded at one end and bent at the other. Then when finally the plank was in place, the "pudding", a length of canvas rolled into a thick wodge would be inserted to caulk it.

An hour went by. The temperatures were soaring down below and by now they were stripped to their underpants, chests lathered in sweat as if they had been greased in Vaseline. The patch was almost half completed and the water in the hold had almost gone. Behind the labouring men, Thirsk and the Engineer, a plump little Scot from Glasgow whom everybody called Mac, even the ordinary hands, were fighting to get the engines re-started again. Time and time again it refused to start. But Mac remained calm, empty pipe stuck out of the corner of his mouth, as he tried yet again. In the end they coaxed the first dry cough from the engine. Time passed. An asthmatic groan followed. More time passed. Suddenly with a ripe juicy belch, the engine burst into full

89

power, the gleaming steel cylinders jerking up and down happily.

Christian, satisfied that everything was going to plan, decided to leave the gang to the patch and go up top.

It was now midday and he knew the men would be hungry. They had been working or on lookout duty for six hours now. So he called up to cook, "Rustle up some bully beef sandwiches and char if you can. The engine's working again. Double quick time. I hope to be underway soon."

"Ay ay, sir," the cook replied cheerfully and disappeared back into his galley to carry out the order. Christian was tempted to have a drink from his flask, but thought better of it in front of the crew. They needed a drink more than he did. Instead he walked around the deck, stopping to chat here and there or say a few words of praise, amazed as always how young the ratings were. A few months before they had been callow youths in cloth caps and "art silk" scarves, solely concerned with "tarts, the pictures and the palais de danse", as they phrased it. Now they were men, hard and lean, carrying out their duties as if they had been at sea for years. He felt a glow of pride in them, telling himself they wouldn't stand conditions like this back in civvy street; they would have long gone on strike.

The cook was just bringing up the big dixie of tea and a bucket filled with corned beef sandwiches when they spotted it: a small black dot on the horizon, which grew steadily larger and when it did, Christian didn't need his aircraft recognition book to know what it was. "Eytie," he announced grimly. "A bloody Eytie reconnaissance flying boat!"

FOUR

Two hundred miles away on the other side of the Mediterranean, Hard and his men raised their heads out of the sand. The Fiesler Storch was turning away now. It hadn't spotted them. He breathed a sigh of relief. They had got away with it yet again. For a minute he thought they had been for the chop. He breathed a sigh of relief and dusting the sand off his knees, as he rose to his feet, he said, "All right, lads, old Jerry's gone."

"Dozy man," Guardsman Smith commented, "idle on parade that's what that Jerry was. He should have spotted us, out in the middle of frigging nowhere."

"Out him on a charge," Sergeant Williams suggested. "Tell Rommel to put him on a fizzer." It wasn't much of a wisecrack, but it broke the tension and the men laughed.

Now they were about five miles south of the coastal road, well beyond the beleaguered port of Tobruk. Soon, Hard knew they'd be striking the German main positions and he guessed that because the Gippos had failed to report that they had dealt with the intruders, the Germans would be expecting them and be on the lookout.

He wiped the sweat off his face with his sleeve. It was furnace hot. Above them the sky was the colour of wood smoke. No wind stirred. Hard shaded his eyes and

91

stared at the midday sun. It was like a copper penny seen dimly at the bottom of a dirty village pond. He shuddered suddenly. He knew what all the signs indicated. They were in for trouble, not from the Germans this time, but from Nature. "All right, lads, have a brew up," he said through cracked parched lips. "I think we're gonna need it."

The men, veterans all, knew what he meant. Wearily and stiffly, they set about making "char" while there was still time. Others tried to urinate, but it was a painful exercise, as hours being jolted up and down in the Dodges.

Hard let them get on with it, as he studied the map of Tobruk and its approaches. For the life of him he couldn't work out which was the best route to infiltrate the German frontline. In the end, he decided first things first. He'd get the patrol across the coastal road and take it from there. There seemed no other alternative.

"Char," Williams broke into his reverie.

"Thanks," Hard answered and took a sip at the scalding hot tea, telling himself as always, that at moments like this, a cup of "sarnt-major's char" tasted better than all the vintage frog champagnes he had ever drunk.

"Penny for them, sir?" Williams asked as they stood there, sipping the brew.

"Just wonder what the best tack is," Hard answered.

Williams looked at the sky. "Well, sir, what's coming might well be a ruddy blessing in disguise." Above him the heavens were getting progressively darker.

Hard sucked his lips thoughtfully. "But how do we know we might not blunder into some Jerry position when it starts?"

"Chance we've got to take, sir. We've taken 'em before."

"Yes, I suppose you're right," Hard answered. "All right, we'll keep on. Tell Dickie Bird to get right on our tail now. We don't want to lose anybody. He can forget convoy distance."

"Right, sir."

A minute later they were on the move again, each man tense and anxious for they knew they were now entering the enemy camp, and if they were taken alive, the Germans would show no mercy after what they had done to the Egyptians. They would be gunned down in cold blood . . .

The sandstorm struck them half an hour later. Abruptly the sun vanished. A gust of wind buffeted the leading Dodge like a blow from a giant fist. The vehicle staggered and for a moment, Guardsman Smith at the wheel thought the engine was going to stall. "All right," Hard bellowed above the sudden howl of the wind, "this is it. We'll keep on going as long as we can." He flung a glance over his shoulder. Dickie Bird in the second Dodge was right on their tail, his headlights on. Hard nodded his approval.

In low gear they continued to grind on, with Hard in the front seat peering anxiously through the growing yellow gloom for the first sight of the enemy.

Minute by minute the wind grew in intensity. Time and time again the lead Dodge was hammered by great gusts that seemed to threaten to overturn. Face set and hard, the sweat trickling down his lean face, Guardsman Smith held on to the wheel with all his strength, his shoulder muscles already burning with the strain and effort. Still they kept on.

Once they saw other lights dimly to the south and Hard

told himself they were probably close to the coastal road. He changed course and they headed northwards ever closer to Tobruk.

Ten minutes later they could go on no longer. At a 100 MPH, the wind hit them in all its hot fury. Like a wall of heated stilettos, the sand particles whipped their faces, making them yelp aloud with the pain. "Hold on to something," Hard yelled urgently. "Don't let yourself go . . . If you start being blown into the desert, you're a gonner . . . We'll never find you—" He couldn't finish. The very words were snatched out of his mouth by that terrible hot wind.

Breathing became difficult. The howling, hellish fog of whirling sand snatched the breath from their lungs. They coughed and gasped desperately like ancient asthmatics. About them as they crouched there fearfully, hanging on for grim death, the ulukating threnody rose to an even fiercer pitch. The wind had travelled a thousand miles from the heart of the Sahara. It wanted to take them and it was not going to be denied its prey. Time and time again it hammered their frail bodies with that hot giant fist.

Once during a slight lull in the terrible storm, Hard raised his head and peered through his sand-caked goggles. For a fleeting moment he thought he glimpsed something. But it was more imagined than seen and then that awesome wind was on them again in full fury. Hurriedly Hard ducked his head and held onto the stanchion with all his strength, as the wind battered his body, trying to force him to relinquish his hold.

With ever renewed force the wind shrieked and howled furiously across the desert as if some cruel god on high had ordained that these puny mortals should be wiped from the face of the earth. It was to be their punishment for their temerity in penetrating his burning kingdom.

Then as suddenly as it had started the *Khamsin* was over. The maddening shrieking howl was replaced by a soft, ever-decreasing dirge. Then it was gone altogether, leaving behind an echo that seemed to go on for ever.

Like sightless men, the patrol felt for their bodies, buried under a layer of warm sand. With his hand Hard cleared the sand from his goggles. He peered short-sightedly at the Guardsman at the wheel. His body was totally encrusted with sand. Hard licked his tongue across his parched lips. A red slash appeared across his face. He shook his head and sat up.

The desert had been transformed, its surface utterly changed by the storm. Stiffly he looked back. The other Dodge was still there. The men were crawling out of it, as if they were infinitely weary, patting the sand from their uniforms. "Sergeant Williams," he called, "Everyone accounted for—" He stopped short.

Only twenty-odd yards away to their right there was a sand-covered Volkswagen jeep with the palm tree and swastika emblem of Rommel's *Afrikakorps* on its corrugated metal side.

"Christ almighty!" Williams cursed, spotting the enemy vehicle in that same instant. "Squareheads."

He forgot the sand and grabbed for his Tommy gun, just in the same moment that Hard tugged out his Colt .45. For already the occupants of the open jeep were attempting to claw their way out. He dropped from the Dodge. Together with Williams he staggered through the deep new sand to the jeep just as the familiar peaked cap of an *Afrikakorps* popped up out of the sand. *"Hande hoch,"* Hard ordered, while Williams covered him with the Tommy gun.

The German shook his head and the sand fell away. He gasped when he saw the two of them there. "Heinz," he said thickly, "*Tommies*!"

The man next to him looked just as startled when he had cleared the sand away and saw the two hard-faced Englishmen standing there with their weapons levelled. "Heaven, arse and cloudburst," he cursed in German and raised his hands.

"Get their weapons and papers," Hard ordered Williams, his mind racing electrically, as the plan began to form in his brain.

"Out you come, Fritz, gildy," Williams commanded and jerked his Tommy gun in the Germans' direction. If they didn't understand the English, the wicked-looking muzzle of the Tommy gun told them all they needed to know. Hastily they got out of the Volkswagen and Williams frisked them while the Guardsmen came across to relieve them of their pistols.

Five minutes later, Hard knew as much about them as he needed to know. They were linesmen out from Rommel's own HQ, which was ten kilometres away. They had been on their way to repair some cables which had come down – and most importantly they knew the password of the day, which surprisingly enough was "*Maus*" in the response to the challenge "Mickey". When Williams heard that, he growled, "I've heard of ruddy daft passwords in my time, but "Mickey-Mouse" takes the frigging candle. Hard had agreed it did.

"Now lads, this is what we're going to do," Hard explained, taking his eyes off the two disheartened prisoners who slumped in the sand next to the jeep under the watchful eye of the Guardsman. "We're about five miles from the Tobruk perimeter – over there." He

96

pointed to the smudge of the horizon, which indicated that Tobruk was being bombed yet again. "At the moment we are just short of the German mainline. I intend to use those two Jerries over there to get us through once it's dusk."

"But do you think they'll co-operate?" Williams asked, slightly alarmed. "They look like tough bastards to me."

"They will all right, Hard said grimly, because I'll be sitting behind them in the jeep. One squawk and they're dead men. Besides I've promised them we'll let them go once we've passed through the German lines."

"I know we've got the passwords and all that, sir," Dickie said. "But what if some other squareheads get suspicious. I mean two Dodges and us." He shrugged and left the rest of his sentence unfinished.

"I've thought of that," Hard answered. "We're going to be Jerry prisoners-of-war that they're bringing in. They've got two rifles in the back of the jeep. We'll use them to pretend we're own guards and the helmets to go with it. There'll be a – er – German guard in each Dodgeload of prisoners."

They grinned and Hard rose from his haunches, the briefing finished. "All right, I suggest we have a brew-up now while it's still light, and we can open those tins of Canadian bacon and some of the bangers as a special treat. All right, get to it."

Squatting in the sand, Dickie Bird said in a mournful voice, "and the condemned man ate a hearty breakfast."

Nobody laughed.

FIVE

It was cold. Overhead a full moon cast its icy white light on the desert, outlining everything a stark black. To their front the flames of Tobruk flickered and died in a silent red. Hard looked at the glowing green dial of his wristwatch. It was nearly ten. He judged the fighting would have died down by now. Strangely enough most battles seemed to be conducted to a strict set of rules. As soon as it got dark, the men were fed and then they settled down to get as much sleep as they could. Most commanders didn't seem to trust their men's ability to fight well at night. It was time to go.

He thrust his pistol into the big German's ribs, "All right, Heinz," he said in German, "move out, and remember." He jerked the pistol harder into Heinz's ribs so that he was well aware of what would happen to him if he played any tricks. Heinz started up. Behind him the drivers of the Dodges did the same. They began to roll.

Thirty minutes passed. Now they were moving at a speedy 20 MPH through the German rear. There were dumps of ammunition, trucks under camouflage nets, artillery batteries everywhere. But no one seemed to take any notice of them. Once they heard a burst of drunken singing, the usual bellowed *"Oh, du schoner Westerwald."* Hard told himself the squareheads must have received their weekly beer ration this night. That was all to the good. If they were blindo they would be less likely, he reasoned, to be interested in the team.

Now they were coming closer to the frontline itself. At regular intervals flares sailed into the night sky, red, green and silver, to hang there for a while colouring the desert an unnatural eerie hue before fluttering to the earth like fallen angels. A couple of times he heard a sharp burst of machine gun fire. German by the sound of it. Yes, they were close to the mainline, he knew that. But fortunately nothing was going on, save that here and there, some sentry was nervous and firing at his own shadow.

They swung round a line of barbed wire, with a dark shape that was the body of a South African soldier, hanging to it. Why he was there, Hard didn't know. Perhaps he was some deserter from the Tobruk garrison, who had run out of luck, been shot in the moment he attempted to surrender. They passed a pit, with a pile of camel shrub around it as camouflage. Inside someone was playing a mouth organ. One of those sickly sentimental tunes they loved. The Germans were always waffling on about their "homeland" and all that trashy sob-story nonsense, Hard told himself.

Now they were slowing down. There were slit trenches everywhere and the driver at the wheel of the jeep had to be careful that he didn't drive into one in the silver darkness.

Hard tensed a little. He knew how the Germans built their lines. They went in for depth unlike the British. There could be up to three lines of slit trenches. They had gone through one line. There could be another two ahead. He peered into the night, a sea of dull unearthly silver, broken only by long shadows and the black masses of rocks and ridges. Above millions of stars blinked and winked. It was like a night in the tropics, Hard thought.

Heinz changed down to second gear as they descended into a wadi. Carefully he swung the wheel to left and right to avoid the rocks which were everywhere. Behind the Volkswagen jeep the two Dodges did the same.

They were half way through the gully when the challenge came, *"Wer da?"*

Hard had been expecting it, but he was startled all the same. That harsh hard voice made him jump. A dark figure was poised against a rock, rifle levelled across the top of it. *"Kennwort?"* the voice demanded.

Hard dug his pistol hard into Heinz's ribs. The sentry wanted the password.

"Mickey," Heinz stuttered and even Hard, who wasn't a fluent German speaker, knew there was something strange about Heinz's voice. He sounded scared. Would the sentry notice?

"Mavs," the sentry answered, but he didn't lower his rifle. Instead he asked in German, "Who's in those trucks? They're Tommy trucks, aren't they?"

"Prisoners," Heinz answered. "We're taking them back."

"Quatsch, Mensch!" the sentry snorted in disbelief. "Have you got all your cups in yer cupboard? You're going the wrong way. What are you doing with Tommy POWs in the main battle line?"

Hard knew they had been rumbled. He took the pistol out of Heinz's ribs and, taking careful aim, as the sentry came out from behind the rock and started to walk towards them with that casual confidence of someone who thinks he is in complete charge of a situation, fired.

At that range he couldn't miss. The big slug caught the

100

sentry squarely in the chest. He shrieked with pain as he was lifted clean off his feet and flung two or three feet backwards. He was dead before he hit the ground.

Almost immediately all hell broke loose. Whistles shrilled, angry voices shouted orders, asked questions. Men started to poke their heads out of holes all around. Tracer zipped wildly back and forth in a sudden panic. Flares hissed into the sky.

"*Dalli!*" Hard yelled urgently at Heinz. "Put your foot down. We're dead men if you don't!"

Heinz needed no urging. He knew what the frontline was like. Men shot first and asked questions afterwards. He pressed the accelerator – hard. The jeep hurtled forward. A German came running out of his hole. His arms were outspread like a child in a school-yard trying to stop another in some boyish game. Heinz didn't hesitate. The man screamed as the jeep struck him. He was screaming still as the wheels crunched over his body. Hard flung a glance behind him. The two Dodges were keeping up. And now the gunners were crouched behind their twin Brownings, firing controlled bursts to left and right. He shook his head. This was bad, he told himself.

A German in a long overcoat reaching almost to his ankles flung a grenade at the jeep. It missed. It exploded in a vicious burst of flame on the far side. Next to the driver the other German screamed hysterically. His left arm had been severed at the shoulder. Now the gaping wound jetted blood furiously. "Stop, I'm hurt!" he pleaded.

"Don't stop. You're dead if you do," Hard commanded. They flew on.

Behind them the two Dodges were zig-zagging the best they could in the narrow wadi, pursued by red tracer like a flight of angry hornets.

They breasted the rise. It was clear now that this whole sector of the German line was in alarm. Men were running everywhere. There was firing from every side. Hard prayed that in the confusion the Germans wouldn't concentrate on the three fleeing vehicles. Streams of tracer hissed to their front. Hard judged them to be about fifty yards away. That must be the last German line. If they could burst it they would be saved.

Suddenly his heart almost stopped. Even above the racket, he could hear the rusty clank of tank tracks – and the only tanks around here, he knew, had to be German. Wildly Hard searched the night for the tank. But even before he found it, the tank – a vicious-looking Mark III – fired. A solid shot, armour-piercing shell hurtled through the night like a glowing golf ball. It hissed just over the top of the jeep and later Hard would always swear, he had felt the heat from it as it had passed and slammed into the rock wall twenty feet away. "Christ!" Hard cursed as the driver swerved instinctively and rammed both front wheels into a large slit trench. The wounded German fell moaning to the ground, while the driver slumped unconscious over the broken wheel.

Hard shook his head. He had taken a nasty bang on his forehead. Red stars were exploding in front of his eyes and there was the coppery taste of blood in his mouth. He felt faint. But he knew he couldn't succumb now. That would be the end of him. He staggered out. Smith in the first Dodge braked to a halt in a flurry of sand. Strong arms grabbed him and tugged him inside as the Mark III tank fired again. Once more that frightening white blob of hard steel hissed through the air. Smith pressed the accelerator down to the floor. The Dodge shot forward. Just in time. The shell whizzed by them harmlessly.

Now they were coming to the end of the German line. To their front, Smith could see the line of posts and although he could not see the skull-and-crossbone sign on them, he knew what they indicated. They were entering the defensive minefield which the Germans had laid in front of their positions, just in case the enemy, the British, counter-attacked. "Fuck this for a tale," he yelled to no one in particular. Grimly he kept on, pursued by the tank's shells and the small arms fire, which was beginning to die away, now that the two vehicles were getting out of range.

"What is it, Smithie?" Hard asked groggily.

"We're in a frigging minefield, sir," Smith answered, not taking his eyes off the ground ahead for one instant.

"Shit!" Hard cursed and prayed that the Germans had not laid anti-tank mines here. If they were only anti-personnel they were all right. They might burst tyres or something, but they would do little harm to the occupants of the Dodges. Anti-tank Teller mines were something else. The ten pounds of high explosive they contained would blow the lot of them to hell and back.

Now as the firing died away, Guardsman Smith concentrated grimly on his task, knowing that really he had no control over the situation. It would be a matter of sheer luck whether they got through the minefield or not. He felt himself beginning to sweat, despite the coldness of the night. A nerve at the side of his face started to twitch out of control. "Christ," he told himself angrily, "don't frigging well crack up now."

They were all expecting it to happen. But when it did, it still came as a shock. Suddenly the ground erupted in front of the truck. The wheels went in a frenzy of shredded rubber. The Dodge sank to its front axle and

103

came to an abrupt halt. "Bale out," Hard cried, "but be careful. After me now!"

Seizing the spade from the side of the truck, as the other Dodge came to a halt behind the wrecked vehicle, Hard started to advance slowly, prodding the ground in front of him with the blade of the shovel. Behind him came the others, carefully keeping in Hard's footprints, while the truck followed them.

The sweat started to pour down Hard's face. His shirt clung wet and warm, to his back. His heart raced. He knew one wrong step and he might well be minus a foot.

Suddenly, startlingly, the blade of the shovel struck metal. "Halt," he commanded in a voice he hardly recognised as his own. He bent. Gingerly he started to clear the sand from the mine. It was an anti-personnel; one of the old-fashioned metal type. He groped his fingers underneath it to check if it were booby-trapped or linked to another mine by wire. It wasn't. Now, with fingers that shook badly, he underscrewed the detonator cap and took out the detonator. "All right," he said thickly, "let's get on with it. It's safe now."

Thus they progressed across the minefield, a group of badly frightened men, lathered in sweat, each one of them wrapped in a cocoon of his own apprehensions. It seemed to take an eternity. It was as if the minefield would go on for ever and ever.

But then a hard voice yelled in English, "Stop where you are, the lot o' yer! We've got yer covered with three Brens."

Hard's knees almost gave beneath him. They had reached the British frontline!

SIX

"Good morning, Miss Stein," Dr Smits said cheerfully.

Lisa took her eyes off a group of South African' who were staggering about drunkenly, although it had just turned dawn, and looked at the doctor. As always, whenever she and Professor Challenger had met him in the last few days – and they had met him quite frequently for a busy military doctor – he was carrying a case over his shoulder. She presumed that it must contain his medical gear. "Good morning," she answered. "You're out early. Doctor."

"Catching a breath of air before the morning hate starts. The Jerries'll be bombarding us with their artillery, as usual, soon enough," he said with a little sigh. "People of routine – the Germans."

"Yes, I know," she answered without thinking.

He looked at her sharply. "You know Germany and the Germans?" he asked.

She avoided answering. Instead she pointed at the drunken Southern African soldiers who were now staggering down the quay, singing their *Stella Marais*. "Is that allowed?" she asked.

Dr Smits shrugged his narrow shoulders. "Of course, it isn't. But their officers are losing control. General Kipper," he meant the commander of the South African division defending Tobruk, "doesn't hold out much hope of successfully defending Tobruk when the Jerries attack in strength, I have been told."

Lisa felt a cold finger of fear trade its way down the small of her back. She shuddered involuntarily. "I hope that won't happen. I don't want to be taken prisoner."

Smits gave her a quick smile, though his sharp dark eyes didn't light up. "Nothing will happen to you. After all you *are* a civilian. By the way, what are two civilians doing here in Tobruk? I hadn't thought of asking before. Well, my dear miss, what are you— "

"Good morning, Dr Smits," Professor Challenger's great booming voice cut into Smits' words. He turned startled. Challenger was looking down at him, clad only in a pair of shorts, his hair still tousled from the sea, a towel draped around his hairy chest. "Thought that now water is getting short, I'd take a dip in the sea before the Hun starts his usual morning hate."

Smits looked displeased. "Don't think I'd use that word any more," he said.

"What word?"

"Hun. The Jerries won't like it when they— "

"Stuff and nonsense," Challenger boomed. "What do I care what the *Huns*," he emphasised the word deliberately, "think? I'd just like to see them tackling me." He frowned threateningly and at his side Lisa smiled. She knew the Germans of old, but it would take more than the Gestapo to frighten Professor Challenger. Suddenly she felt safe and protected again.

Down the quayside the drunken South Africans were throwing stones at the black labourers working, as usual, waist-deep in the water, trying to salvage what they could from the wrecked vessel. "Kaffir pack!" they were yelling.

"Wait the Germans come – they'll cut your tails off for good. Ha . . . ha . . ."

"What a mob!" Professor Challenger exploded. "Totally out of control." He fixed Smits with a hard look. "Can't you do something, Smits? You're an officer after all."

Smits shrugged weakly. "I don't think, in the state they are in, they will listen to me, especially as I'm a medical corps wallah."

Challenger looked at him. That use of "wallah" seemed strange in a South African. It was usually the old sweats in the British Army, who used such terms, with their bits and pieces of languages they had picked up during their service all over the Empire – their "bints", "bondhooks", "gildy" and all the rest of it. He frowned. He opened his mouth to say something, but before he could a motor-cycle, driven at high speed by a staff officer, came whizzing down the quay to brake in a squeal of protesting rubber and a flurry of white dust next to them. "Professor Challenger and Dr Stein?" the young officer queried.

"Yes," Challenger said gravely. "I am he. And this is Dr Stein."

The officer touched his hand to his battered cap. "You're wanted at HQ, sir. Immediately. I've been sent to fetch you at once."

"Where's the fire?" Challenger asked, as Smits watched, his brow furrowed in a puzzled frown.

"Don't know, sir," the young officer replied. "Just my chief, Colonel Mackay of Intelligence, told me to bring the two of you to HQ – tootsweet." He flung the door of the sidecar open. "Here you are, Miss. Bit tight. But you'll manage it, I'm sure."

"Thank you." She clambered into the sidecar with

107

difficulty, revealing a delightful glimpse of her inner thigh, which made the young officer's eyes sparkle.

Challenger threw him a threatening look before he mounted the pillion seat, while Smits stared at the two of them curiously, hand held to the box slung over his back, as if he were reassuring himself that it was still there. "See you later perhaps," Smits said, as the staff officer kick-started the motorbike.

"Wouldn't bank on it, old chap," the officer said cheerfully. Then he was turning in a quick circle and roaring back the way he had come, leaving Smits to sort out the puzzle. What was so important about these two civilians, one of whom was obviously of German origin, that an officer had been sent to bring them back to the head of British Intelligence in Tobruk? In the end he decided that he didn't know the answer, but that he had better report the information to the Count. Count von Almaszy might be able to put the pieces of the jigsaw together and come up with the answer. He was a cunning old fox after all. Looking to left and right to see if the coast was clear and finding that it was, Dr Smits slipped into the nearest ruined house and started to take out the transmitter from the bag on his back . . .

"All the signs are that Rommel will start an all-out attack on Tobruk in the next forty-eight hours," Colonel Mackay, a big bluff officer, who had a patch over the empty socket of his left eye, lectured them. "He's got his guns in place and he seems to be massing his tanks to the south-east – here around the road to El Adem and the other road leading south-east to the Egyptian frontier."

Hard nodded his understanding, while Challenger and Dr Stein looked a little uneasy at this kind of military briefing which was unfamiliar to them.

"The Indian Brigade is holding the line in that area – because between you and me . . ." He looked furtively at the blanket which covered the cave which was his HQ, "the South Africans haven't got the moral strength to do the job. They're about finished in my opinion," he added gravely, looking very serious.

Challenger, remembering what he had seen of the South Africans only an hour before, nodded his agreement. "Can't someone put a stiffener in them?" he asked. "Give 'em a bit of backbone?"

"'Fraid not, Professor," Mackay answered. "From top to bottom, the whole division seems to have lost its will to fight. Last year the Aussies and us held this place successfully for months. But the Springboks won't. Well, as I was saying. If the attack comes in from the south-east, as I anticipate it will, and the Germans break through the Indians, then they'll be faced with the British Brigade – Coldstream Guards, Sherwood Foresters and the Worcesters, who hold the centre not far from the NAAFI – here. They'll hold, I think. But then, if Rommel attacks the South Africans – here – and they break, which they will, the three British infantry regiments won't stand a chance. It could be all over in a matter of days," he shrugged in a resigned manner, "perhaps even hours."

Hard sucked his teeth. Mackay was pessimistic like most Intelligence officers Hard had ever known.

Outside there came the rumble of artillery and the blanket flapped back and forth suddenly as the first enemy shells detonated. Mackay fixed his smoked glass monocle more firmly in his eye and listened intently. "The morning hate," he announced after a while. "But it seems heavier than normal." He pursed his lips. "This could be it – the softening up barrage."

109

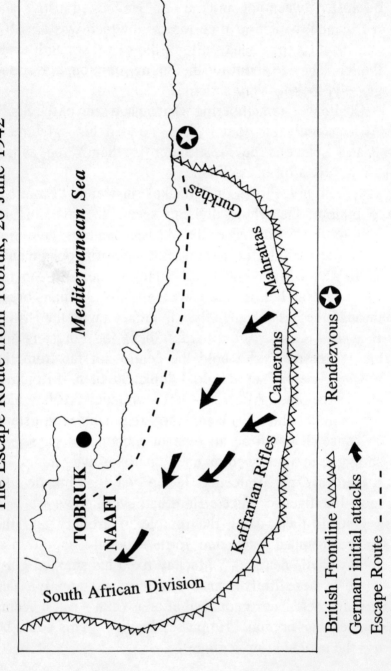

The Escape Route from Tobruk, 20 June 1942

Mediterranean Sea

TOBRUK

NAAFI

South African Division

Gurkhas

Mahrattas

Camerons

Kaffrarian Rifles

Rendezvous

British Frontline ︿︿︿︿︿
German initial attacks ➤
Escape Route – – –

"Then we should get out of here as soon as possible, sir," Hard said.

"Exactly. But you'll have to wait till nightfall. You wouldn't stand a chance in daylight. Not now, with Rommel massing the whole of Afrika Korps and his Italian divisions around Tobruk."

"Agreed, sir. And we're not quite ready. We've not found the extra vehicle we need to replace the Dodge and then there's the business of signalling the captain of the *Black Swan*.

"That's been taken care of already, Major," Mackay said.

"Thank you, sir."

"Not at all. But let me say this. You are an experienced officer. You know just before a battle, everything's in place and the situation is tight. Once the battle begins, however, things become fluid – men are too busy fighting their own bit of the battle and staying alive, he added cheerfully, "to notice what other people are up to. In other words, it's a kind of controlled chaos."

"Yessir, I know."

"Well, if I were going to break out of here, I think I'd wait till the battle had started. I think I'd stand a better chance of getting away then."

Hard said, "I suppose you're right, sir," and Challenger looked at the one-eyed Intelligence man and asked, "And what about you, Colonel? What are you going to do when the balloon goes up?"

Mackay didn't reply for a moment, then he said, "Well, we of the 8th Army have done far too much running over these last years. I, for one, have decided I'm not going to do any more running." He tapped the revolver at his belt. "I might be a one-eyed cripple, but

I can still shoot straight. I'll join the Coldstreamers, I think."

Challenger nodded grimly. "I see what you mean," he said.

The one-eyed Colonel forced a grin, "Well, I won't keep you any longer. You'll have a lot to do before this day is over."

In the next cave the phones started to ring urgently and they could hear the muffled voice of a staff officer saying petulantly, "But you must hold out, I tell you. Do you hear, it's vital you hold out!"

Colonel Mackay said, "Well, there you are. It's started, gentlemen – and hm, lady. Rommel's marched."

Challenger flashed a look at Lisa. There was a glint of tears in her eyes. He knew why. They were going and the Colonel was going to die here. Gruffly he took her arm and said, "Come on, my dear. We're in the way here now . . ."

SEVEN

"What do you think, Chiefie?" Christian asked Thirsk, as he scanned the horizon. It was an hour now since the Fiat seaplane had spotted them and still nothing had happened.

Thirsk at the wheel gave a little shrug. "The Eyetie probably saw we were in a bit of a pickle, sir," he replied. "They knew they can take their time. But they'll be after us in the end. The Eyeties don't tend to tackle anything tough. We'll look like easy heat to them. Hell's teeth, we're not doing more than five knots an hour."

"Yes," Christian said a little gloomily. "I suppose you're right. But we can't be that far off Gib now. Perhaps the Rock can send us air cover?"

"Ay, sir. If only we could send them a signal. But, as you know, Sparks sez the radio's on the bleeding blink as well."

"Hm. Anyway we'll just have to keep bashing on regardless."

"'Spect you're right, sir," Thirsk agreed, though there was no enthusiasm in his voice.

Another hour passed. Now the sun was high in the sky, casting a warm yellow glow over the perfect, calm blue sea. It was something for which Christian was grateful. The calmness of the sea placed no great strain on the patch, as did the "Mucky Duck"'s low speed. Any surge in speed, as in evasive action, he told himself, would put a lot of pressure on the patch. He prayed that things would go on like they were at this moment . . .

"Stand by, engine room," *Leutnant zur See* Bastian ordered. He raised his glasses once again and focused on the ship some two kilometres away. It had to be the ship the spaghetti-eater pilot had reported he had sighted. A rusty old Tommy tug with a single high funnel rolling from side to side awkwardly, as if the helmsman were blind drunk. "Easy meat," the cocky young E-boat skipper, with his white cap tilted at a a rakish angle, told himself. One tin fish and she'd be finished. It'd be as easy as falling off a log.

He ran his glasses the length of the old-fashioned tug and spotted the great jagged hole which had been plugged from inside. "So that's the reason why," he told himself, speaking to himself in the fashion of lonely men.

He lowered his binoculars and threw a dash of cheap cologne over the white silk muffler, which he affected, to take away the E-boat's permanent stench of fuel oil and metal. "Bridge here," he rasped, "let me have full ahead – both."

There was a muffled reply from the engine room and Bastian tensed at the controls for what was soon to come.

Suddenly the deck pulsated and vibrated under his feet. He held on to the controls with a tightened grip. The prow tilted. Behind them the screws raced. A great white wake of water flew up to both sides. Bastian felt that old thrill as the E-boat surged forward. *Twenty knots . . . twenty-five . . . thirty knots.*

"*Stand by, tube one . . . tube two!*" he yelled.

The two torpedo mates bent over the weapons at each side of the bow.

Leutnant zur See Bastian grinned. The Tommy was in for a nasty surprise in a minute or two. He'd put those deadly "kippers" right up his arse. They'd make his eyes pop.

On the deck the torpedo mates in their leather jackets were soaked by the flying spray now, but they were alert and ready to fire. Bastian glanced to his front. The tug seemingly had still not spotted him. Now he started counting off the range . . . 1000 metres . . . 700 . . . 500 . . . Close enough. He cupped his hands around his mouth and bellowed, *"Fire one!"*

The portside torpedo mate fired the weapon. The boat lurched slightly as the one-ton torpedo plunged over the side. There was a sudden flurry of bubbles and then it was speeding away in a streak of white.

"Fire two!"

Another of the deadly fish slid into the water and raced for the tug.

Hastily Bastian raised his binoculars, feeling his hands tremble with suppressed excitement as he did so. There was no hope for the Tommy now, he told himself as he swept the glasses the length of the tug's battered hull.

In a moment, Bastian thought, the Tommy's tiny steel world could erupt in a flash of angry red and yellow flame and come to a sudden violent end. He waited tensely for the explosion.

Nothing happened!

Bastian flung glance below to the two torpedo mates. They looked back at him in utter bewilderment, too. Both "kippers" had failed to explode. For a minute Bastian did not know what to do. But the sudden stream of white tracer zipping lethally across the still waters told him he had to act. He swung the E-boat round in a tremendous curve of wild white and told himself angrily that someone had sabotaged the damned "kippers". Still the Tommy was not going to get away. Now he was more determined than ever to send her to the bottom of the sea.

"Starboard thirty!" Christian yelled as the torpedoes hit the hill with the great hollow boom of steel striking steel. "Engine room can you make smoke? We're being attacked!"

"Christ almighty!" Thirsk cursed at the wheel, as thick black smoke started to pour almost immediately from the "Mucky Duck's" single stack.

Christian flung up his glasses as the smoke started to descend to sea level. The lean shape of the German E-boat slid knifelike into the circles of calibrated glass. A great white bow wave flew up from her stern. Her starboard guard rails were nearly underwater as she raced in for another attack.

"Stand by for torpedoes!" Christian yelled as below the gunner at the "Chicago piano" fired a furious salvo at the E-boat which was now zig-zagging to left and right as it came in, ready to destroy this impertinent little tug.

Bastian was taking no more chances. He had shoved the blond midshipman from behind the Vierling four-barrelled 20mm flak cannon himself. As the E-boat surged ever closer to the smoke-shrouded target, he pressed the elevator pedal. The four, air-cooled slim barrels sank immediately. The blur of smoke raced into the ring sight of the cannon. Laughing wildly, carried away by the primeval lust to kill, he pressed the trigger.

Crazily the four cannon started to pound away. White tracer shells raced through the air. They riveted a line of jagged holes along the tug's superstructure.

116

Behind the bridge, the gunner at the twin Brownings, screamed shrilly and fell dangling from his perch, his face shot away with his jawbone gleaming like polished ivory in the bright scarlet welter of blood and gore. "Keep control." Christian yelled at the Thirsk. "I'll man the guns."

Before Thirsk had time to protest, Christian had swung himself out of the bridgehouse and with surprising agility for a bulky, middle-aged man had flung himself into the dead gunner's seat.

Next instant the twin Brownings started to chatter again. Christian saw the spurts of water where his slugs were striking home. He was firing short. Desperately he upped the range, as yet another burst of 20mm shell fire ripped the length of the "Mucky Duck". A rating screamed and went over the side, arms flailing wildly, as he attempted to save himself – and failed.

"*Fuck it*," Christian cried and bit his bottom lip till the blood came, firing all out.

In the bridgehouse, CPO Thirsk prayed as he zig-zagged to port and then to starboard, half blinded by the smoke still pouring from the tug's stack, desperately trying to save the "Mucky Duck". He had been sunk at Jutland in 1916 as a boy and had been in the water for fourteen hours. Then, despite the freezing cold of the North Sea, he had known he was going to live. Now, he felt he was about to die. What chance did the old tub stand against the high-speed most modern torpedo boat in the world? "*The Lord be my shepherd*," he repeated the old prayer, "*I shall not want— *"

When help came, it did so from a totally unexpected quarter. The two big flying boats came in almost silently. It was their usual tactic against surface craft. Throttles cut back, engines muted, they glided down on the E-boat out of the blood-red sun.

Bastian heard them when it was too late. He tugged up the anti-aircraft cannon. But already the first of the Sunderland flying boats of Coastal Command bombs were falling out of the sky, they missed. They straddled the E-boat to port and starboard. Huge jets of water erupted to both sides of her. The E-boat reeled back and forth. Her radio mast seemed to touch the blue water. But the bombs of the second four-engined flying boat didn't miss. The first bomb hit the German craft amidships. A gout of red flame erupted at once. It fanned the whole length of the torpedo boat.

"You've hit the jackpot, skipper," the tail gunner yelled over the intercom as the flying boat soared over the E-boat. "Right on the gas tanks. *She's frigging well going up!*"

What followed the crews of the two Sunderlands would never forget. Men on fire. Insane human torches. Men thrashed their uniforms with burning hands, trying in vain to put out the flames. Men screaming silently, whose flesh was bubbling and blackening on their frames while they were still alive. Men lying on the burning decks being charred and shrunken to the size of pygmies. Men in their dying agony arching their spines, hands flung out, as if they were nailed to a cross in some latter-day crucifixion. Men dying . . .

Bastian dived over the side. At Mürwik as a cadet he had been the best swimmer in his year. Now he struck out crazily from the burning sinking ship. Ten metres . . . twenty metres . . . thirty . . . he was escaping that great roaring inferno. But he was not to escape. Suddenly there was a huge explosion. Flames jetted a hundred feet into the air. Next instant tons of burning fuel oil slapped down to the surface of the sea. It engulfed Bastian. The water steamed and bubbled and he went under burning and drowning in the same instant. Next moment what was left of his craft slid below the surface of the sea.

A minute or too later the first of the two Australian flying boats landed next to the battered "Mucky Duck". A dinghy was lowered and the second pilot rowed across to the tug. He looked up at Christian's bearded face, the blood trickling down his cheek where he had been wounded. "Anyone for us to take back to Gib, skipper?" he yelled.

Christian shook his head. "We've two dead – that's about it."

The Australian looked the length of thr tug, with its shattered mast and holed hull. "The two of us could manage the crew if you want to open the seacocks and sink her," he suggested.

"*Sink* her man!" Christian roared. "Why the *Black Swan* is good for another fifty years at least."

The young Australian grinned. "Have it your way, skipper. We'll be going then. But Gib's got you on their radar now, so you'll be OK. Look us up when you get there, we'll buy you some grog, skipper."

Christian shook his head and said, "No sir, *we'll* be buying the grog. And thanks."

EIGHT

The telegraph clattered one more time and the engine stopped. But there was no silence, for on both sides of the dock, the civilians and the sailors in their blue dungarees cheered and cheered. Christian frowned. What was there to cheer about? The old "Mucky Duck" had taken a bad beating. CPO Thirsk, however, was moved. He rubbed a bony finger in his eyes in which there was the glint of tears. "Who'd 'a' bloody thought it, he murmured to no one in particular, "cheering the ruddy old "Mucky Duck" like that!"

The box-like ambulance rumbled up and the wounded were swung ashore by cradle. "What about yer dead?" the ROMC sergeant shouted across, voice cold and unfeeling despite the cheering all around.

Christian flashed him a hard look. Then he caught himself. The NCO was just doing his duty. Perhaps he dealt with dead men every day. "Buried them at sea, the way all sailors should be buried," he said and then spotting the jeep, flying the flag of the Governor, nosing its way through the cheering mob, he jumped over to the quayside. "Chiefie," he called over his shoulder, "look after things. I think my presence is being requested."

It was. A handsome young staff captain got out of the jeep and said, "Quayle, Captain Quayle. You're wanted at

Government House immediately, Lieutenant. The balloon is apparently about to go up."

The Governor, a hard-faced general with clever eyes, briefed him personally over a whisky and soda, sitting there in the big room with the ceiling fan stirring the warm air above their heads. "Christian, I used to be in Intelligence, so they've let me in a bit on this one. Everyone from the PM downwards is screaming for action. Apparently the balloon's about to go up in Tobruk and the people the PM wants to get out are to move soon."

He gave Christian a hard look and was tempted to ask him why the Prime Minister was so concerned about the fate of two civilians, but then he thought better of it and didn't.

"Is Major Hard there?" Christian asked and took a deep drink of his whisky, telling himself as he did so, he'd not drunk a drop of alcohol for over twenty-four hours. Strange!

"Yes," the governor answered. "The Hard Long Range Group got through safely. Now the problem is getting them out again. But first things first. What's the state of your craft and its crew?"

Christian finished his glass and looked pointedly at the bottle of Haig, but the governor didn't seem to notice. He gave a little sigh and said, "The *Black Swan's* pretty battered, sir. Her hull has been holed and the superstructure has been knocked about a bit."

The governor made a swift note on the pad in front of him. "The dockies will start work on her as soon as we are finished here. And the crew?"

"Lost two men killed and two wounded."

"Can you manage without them?"

"I need a gunner, sir, that's all," Christian answered. "I prefer not to take any new crew on board at this stage."

"Good." Again the governor made a note on his pad. "I'll have a gunner sent over from the coast artillery immediately. Now we'll resupply you and fill you up with any ammo you might need. Anything special?"

"Yessir," Christian answered, visualising the small natural harbour where he would rendezvous with Hard and his party.

"Tommy guns for every member of my crew. Where we're going we could just run in trouble where we'd need every bit of fire power possible."

The governor frowned. "Tall order," he said. "These days everyone wants Tommy guns." Again he made a swift note. "But you shall have them, Christian." He gave the other man a tight smile. "Now then I'll leave you in charge of Captain Quayle outside. You have quarters here in Government House. I'll arrange for your crew to be fed and bathed ashore, too. Give 'em a bit of a rest. I hear they've been through a hard time."

Christian nodded and asked, "How much time have we got, sir?"

The governor's smile changed to a frown. "Twenty-four hours at the most," he answered. "The pressure's on. All right, Christian, have a good rest. Anything you want just ask for it from Quayle. You're to be given – what's that new American thing? – yes, the very important person treatment. VIP. I'll keep you in the picture, if anything comes. If I don't see you again, then good luck." He stretched out his hand and Christian shook it.

Outside Quayle was waiting for him, a roguish smile on his handsome face. "Your bath's running. We've scrounged a clean shirt and a pair of underpants of about your size. "I'm afraid we can't provide dancing girls – they're a bit rare in Gib. But we do have this for you, Lieutenant." He pulled his hand from behind his back. In it he had clasped a litre bottle of whisky. "That'll keep you happy in your bath, I have no doubt." His grin vanished. "Just one thing, however."

"Yes," Christian answered taking the bottle gratefully.

"The Governor says you should keep under cover as much as possible. The Huns are very present here on the mainland. Their spies watch everything going in and out of Gib and your "Muck" – er – *Black Swan*— "

"You can call her the "Mucky Duck" if you like, Captain," Christian interrupted. "We all do."

Quayle returned his grin. "Well, as I've said, the "Mucky Duck" has attracted a great deal of attention as it is all that cheering and the like. We don't want the Huns to think they're on to something important and come gunning for you again when you sail, do we?"

Christian shrugged a little carelessly. "I'll worry about that eventuality when it comes up. Now point me in the direction of that bathroom – and, oh yes, I'll need a glass, a very large one."

"And you shall have it. Come along, skipper . . ."

Swiftly von Almaszy read the message from Spain and pursed his wrinkled old lips. It was all fitting together now. That business in Egypt, the two civilians inside Tobruk less than five kilometres away, the killers of the Long Range Desert Group and now the hero's welcome for the tug, commanded by the same man who had met Hard in Cairo, in Gibraltar.

He tugged the end of his long nose, thoughtfully. Everything indicated that the two civilians, Professor

Challenger and a Dr Stein, as Smits had reported their names, were important enough for Churchill to have ordered their rescue, cost what it may. *But how are they damned important*? a harsh little voice rasped at the back of his mind.

He pondered the matter for some time, while outside his tent the guns continued to thunder prior to the coming attack. Tanks rumbled by clattering noisily to their positions. They were followed by Italian infantry who shuffled by, hang-dog looks on their dark faces and without enthusiasm. Von Almaszy knew why. Rommel would use them as cannon-fodder in the first assault wave. When they had tested the Englishmen's strength, Rommel's elite German infantry would follow.

In the end, von Almaszy gave up. He couldn't solve the puzzle. But he knew something had to be done. Those two civilians had to be taken alive and the Hard group punished for what they had done to the Egyptians. Nassar and the other plotters would demand it.

Five minutes later he was standing in front of Rommel's makeshift desk. The Desert Fox looked harassed and hot. Both his bare arms were covered with desert sores now and he had a dirty bandage wrapped around a particularly large one on his right arm. "I can give you five minutes at the most, von Almaszy," he snapped curtly. He waved through the open tent flap at the troop-filled desert outside. "Things are moving at top speed, as you can see. Time is running out."

"I'll be brief, Excellency," the aged officer said. "I want your permission to take my Brandenburgers into Tobruk just before the attack starts – say – two hours or so beforehand."

"Why?" Rommel snapped.

Hastily von Almaszy explained the importance of the two civilians inside the besieged port, while Rommel scowled, as if the other man was wasting his time at this crucial stage of the campaign. Von Almaszy saw the scowl and added quickly, "We must show our Egyptian friends that we are prepared to help them by dealing with that murderer Hard and his bunch of desert thugs. After all, Your Excellency, in a week's time we might well be in Cairo and *we* will then need the help of the Egyptians. It will make it much easier for the German Army to rule Egypt if we have the co-operation of the Egyptian army and others who have aided us."

That clinched it. Rommel nodded his head. "Yes, we give our permission for you and the Brandenburgers to go in first. Briefly, how will you do it?"

"From the south-east, sir. We'll use captured Tommy vehicles."

"That's the direction from which I shall launch my initial assault before having a crack at the South Africans. Two-pronged assault, in other words."

"Yessir. And to the south-east is the way that Hard party will try to escape. I am sure of it. It is the most logical route for them. They'll head for Egypt that way or my feeling is that this boat of theirs might well attempt to pick them up further along the coast. That's why I'd like to capture them while I know exactly where they are – Tobruk."

"All right then, von Almaszy. The assault goes in at first light tomorrow morning. That will be zero five-thirty hours. I suggest that you and your people go in exactly two hours beforehand at zero three. The moon will have vanished by then, the Met people tell me, and as you know the Tommies are creatures of routine. They won't be expecting trouble at that time for they always, invariably stand to at dawn."

"Thank you, Your Excellency," von Almaszy said and clicking to attention, gave the Desert Fox an awkward salute.

In spite of the tension of the coming battle Rommel laughed and said, "Well, I hope you're a better fighting soldier, von Almaszy, than you are a parade-ground one. Well, off you go – and *Hals und Beinbruch*."*

Outside von Alamszy looked at Tobruk. Already it was beginning to grow dark. Long shadows were slipping across the desert like silent hawks. He nodded, as if agreeing with some inner voice. This night he'd deal with Hard and his gangsters for good. Then he hurried off to brief his Brandenburgers.

* Literally, break your neck and leg, i.e. happy landings.

NINE

Lisa Stein tossed and turned on the camp bed in the hot tent. She was dreaming. Hard had insisted she should take a mild sedative so that she could rest before the ordeal to come. Now she was back at the border station at Emmerich in 1937, the day she had left Germany for good.

"*Alles aussteigen*," the station master in his red cap had yelled officiously and the travellers to Holland had got out obediently under the watchful eyes of the border guards with the Alsatian dogs and big automatics on their hips.

"*Passkontrolle*," another official had shouted and together with the rest, subdued and frightened as they all were, she had shuffled towards the border guard sitting at the high desk, ignoring the steam coming from the chuntering locomotive, bespectacled gaze flashing from the passports to the big ledger next to him. She knew what that was. Other Jews who had already fled the Third Reich had told her. It was the black book. In it were the names of those who faced automatic arrest, if they were apprehended. She was not in it. But her position was just as bad. For in her passport, stamped in red, was a single letter, "*J*" for Jewess. She, too, faced special treatment, she knew that.

She came level with the man in the spectacles. He

127

flipped open the first page, saw the red stamp and, with a bored jerk of his thumb, motioned to a little shack at the side of the platform. "Jewess in there – for special examination."

Swallowing her anger at the treatment, she walked to the shack, which she now saw had been built above the station toilet. She opened the door and was met by the odour of disinfectant and stale urine. A hard-faced woman, with her hair tugged severely back into a bun, stood there arms folded over a massive bosom. "Jewess?" she rapped.

Numbly Lisa had nodded. The woman handed her a paper cup immediately. "Drink this," she ordered. "It's castor oil. Then go and crap over there in the bucket . . . in that cubicle."

Lisa could have shrieked, but she kept calm. She knew what the Nazis wanted. They wanted to see if she was trying to smuggle out precious stones in her gut. Obediently she started for the cubicle after drinking the foul-tasting oil.

"Oh, and strip naked," the woman added. "I have to search your clothes. Then I'll do you."

"Yes," she answered dully, trying to keep her temper. Her cheeks burned with indignity of it all. Yet she knew it would be over in an hour or so and then she would be on her way to Holland and from there to England, leaving the accursed Hitler's Germany behind her.

She felt her bowels begin to heave. Hurriedly she ripped off her clothes and sat on the bucket. Only the Nazis could think up something like this, she told herself as her bowels rumbled and groaned.

"Are you finished, Jewess?" the hard-faced woman with the bun asked a little while later.

"Yes," she answered weakly, feeling nauseated and drained.

"Step out then," the woman commanded. *"Naked."*

She drew aside the blanket and stepped out of the cubicle. The woman eyed her coldly. "Raise your arms," she commanded.

Obediently Lisa had raised her arms.

The woman came close to her. Lisa wrinkled her nostrils in disgust. The woman had a penetrating, unwashed smell. Roughly she felt Lisa's ampits and then underneath her breasts.

"Lower your arms," she commanded.

Lisa had done so and then she had run her thick fingers through Lisa's hair.

"Spread your legs."

Lisa had hesitated. Hadn't she been humiliated enough?

"I said, spread your legs!" the woman barked harshly. "They tell me you Yid women like spreading them as it is at every available opportunity." The woman had laughed coarsely, as Lisa had done as she had been ordered.

The woman poked a finger in her vagina. She had done it roughly and her nail was sharp. She had winced and the woman had laughed again. "What did you expect – Vaseline and kid gloves?" the woman had mocked. "All right, Yid, you can get dressed now. I'll check your shit later."

Hurriedly Lisa had begun to reach for her clothes piled on the three-legged stool, but the harsh male voice had stopped her in her tracks. "Don't move, Jewess," it had commanded.

Her hands had flown to her naked breasts, as she had seen the man standing there in the doorway, unlit cigar gripped between his thick sensual lips, his eyes assessing her naked body greedily.

The man had Gestapo written all over him. He was dressed in an ankle-length green leather overcoat, with a dark hat pulled well down over his brow, as if he wanted to hide his fat vile face.

A moment later she had known she was right when he had said to the woman, "Leave us. I want to examine the Jewess personally."

The woman had looked up at the fat-faced man for a moment as though she might refuse to go, then she had said tamely, *"Jawohl, Herr Oberkommissar"*, and had gone out, leaving the two of them alone.

Slowly, deliberately, working the unlit cigar stump from one side of his fat mouth to the other, the Gestapo man had unbuttoned his leather coat. For years later she had recalled how the leather had creaked as he had done so.

"Come here," he had said then, not taking his greedy eyes off her naked body for instant.

She had crossed to the room to where he was standing as if in a trance, knowing that something bad was going to happen, but knowing, too, that she could do nothing to stop it. She was fully in the power of this evil man.

Next moment the Gestapo man made it quite clear that she was.

"Listen, Jewess," he said, hand held in front of his flies. "Understand this. I can do with you what I want." He rolled the cigar to the other side of his mouth. "I have power of life or death over your kind. One word from me and you'll be for the camps. Do you realise that?"

Not trusting herself to speak, she had nodded mutely and had tensed for what was to come.

"Now I am not going to soil my honest German prick by sticking it in a Jewess." He had grinned evilly at what

130

he thought was something funny. "However, Jewess, I do fancy a little bit of pleasure on a dull Tuesday like today." Slowly, deliberately, he had begun to unbutton his flies, not taking his gaze off her for a minute.

She had felt herself start to tremble, her eyes darting back and forth like those of a trapped animal.

He had finished unbuttoning his flies. He had reached in his fat paw and had brought out his organ, ugly and misshapen but already half erect. "Take a good look at it, Jewess," he had commanded, his voice thick with lust now. "That's the only piece of good German salami you'll ever see again in your lifetime . . . *Kneel!*"

She felt she would faint. Only by an effort of conscious will-power had she been able to do as he had ordered.

He had looked down at her contemptuously. "That's where all you Jewish whores should be," he had sneered, "*on their knees!*" Suddenly he had grabbed her roughly by the hair and tugged her towards him. "Now suck!" Next instant he had filled her mouth with that revolting thing of his . . .

"*Lisa . . . Lisa.*" Challenger's voice, concerned and soft (for him) seemed to come from a long way off.

She shook her head and opened her eyes, that awful picture receding rapidly from her mind's eye.

"You were moaning and groaning in your sleep," Challenger said and now she could see him in the faint light of the moon, coming through the open flap of the tent, "saying something in German which I couldn't understand. But it sounded awful."

Instinctively she wiped the back of her hand, which was trembling, across her lips. There was nothing there.

Challenger stroked her sweating forehead tenderly, "You're all right now, Lisa, aren't you?" he asked, his

131

bearded face worried. "I'll look after you. You'll be safe with me – and Major Hard."

She took his hand and kissed it.

Challenger looked surprised. "I say!" he boomed.

"Thank you," she whispered, the horror of that afternoon at the border station gone now. "I know you'll look after me, I've always known that ever since we set off on our journey."

"Thank God, you're all right," Challenger said and stood up at the side of her cot. "Probably the sedative and the worry about what's to come must have triggered off some kind of nightmare."

"I expect so," she agreed because she didn't want to tell him what had really happened at Emmerich. She knew that with his violent temper, any German who fell into his hands then wouldn't live to tell the tale. "Thank you for being so concerned about me. I'm just silly, that's all."

"Be as silly as you like to be, Lisa," Challenger said. "As long as you're not unhappy. I never want you to be unhappy again." Awkwardly he patted her hand with his great hairy paw and Lisa realised that a new and different kind of bond had been forged between her and "old Lost World".

"Major Hard has just told me we shall be moving out in about an hour. So I suppose you'd better get yourself ready, Lisa."

She nodded her understanding.

"Oh and by the way that Intelligence colonel chap gave me this for your handbag— " Challenger suddenly looked very embarrassed "—he said just in case." He pulled a small pearl-handled revolver from his pocket, dwarfed in his great palm. "Said, he'd taken from an Eyetie madam, who was running one of their mobile brothels which we captured." Challenger looked even more embarrassed and handed her the little gun as if it were abruptly red hot. "Here you are. Now, I'll leave you to get ready."

"Professor," she said realising suddenly that she didn't even know Challenger's first name, "would you kiss me before you go? Please."

"Gosh," Challenger said in amazement, "I say!"

Outside Smits sucked his teeth. He still didn't know what the importance of these two civilians was. Now the fact that the woman, who wasn't a doctor of medicine, had been talking gibberish in German in her nightmare, puzzled him even more. What in three devils' name were they up to? Slowly, thoughtfully, he walked to the motorcycle, which he had "bought" from a corporal of the Kaffrarian Rifles for two bottles of Cape brandy. When Hard and his killers moved out, he would follow them. Count von Almaszy was making quite sure they weren't going to escape him.

Fifty yards away, Hard finished putting on his equipment. Now he crooked his finger at Sergeant Williams and indicated he should come with him to the back of the three-tonner truck with which Intelligence had supplied the group. Hard pulled out his hip flask and gave it to the NCO. "Take a drink of that – it's good Scotch, none of that Gippo stuff."

In the moonlight Williams' face registered his surprise. But it wasn't every day that he got a chance of a drink of real Scotch whisky. He took the flask gratefully, saying, "Ta, sir." He lifted it to his lips, took a great slug, breathed "ar" and handed it back to Hard with, "That hit the spot, sir."

Hard grinned, though he had never felt less like grinning. "Good," he said. "Now Sarge, you're my

second-in-command, so I have to order you to do this."
He licked his dry cracked lips and looked the sergeant's
open honest face in the silver light of the moon, only
half registering the persistent boom of the German guns
which had been going all day. "If anything happens to
me, you'll be in charge, Sarge. Now I'm going to make
you responsible for carrying out the same order that I
will have to carry out if it seems likely that Professor
Challenger and Dr Stein might fall into enemy hands."

"And what's that, sir?" Williams asked pleasantly, still
savouring the warm glow of the scotch.

"This," Hard's voice turned suddenly very harsh,
"*shoot 'em!*"

Williams looked at him, as if he had suddenly gone
crazy. "Fucking Christ Almighty," he gasped.

TEN

"Better put on my battle bowler," the colonel of Intelligence yelled above the thunder of the guns. He took off his red-banded staff cap and threw it into the night, as if he would never need it again and knew he wouldn't. Then he eased the chin strap of his steel helmet under his chin.

To their front, the sky was alive with signal flares and the cherry-red flames of fires. Somewhere a petrol dump had gone up, struck by one of the German shells and a mushroom of bright scarlet flame was ascending to the moonlit sky.

The colonel patted the top of his helmet to check whether it was sitting correctly and yelled, "You'll be going out through the lines of the Gurkhas. They're closest to the coast and the coastal road which I'm sure the Huns will use when they attack. But I think those fine little chaps are more likely to hold than their neighbours to the right flank – the Mahrattas. The Huns are deadly afraid of the Gurkas and their kurkris."

Hard nodded his understanding and asked, "Have they been warned that we're coming? When the balloon goes up there'll be mass confusion and I wouldn't like to get shot by our own people. It would hurt twice as much."

In the flash of an exploding shell, Hard caught the grin

135

on the colonel's face, though his faded, bloodshot eyes still remained worried. "I'm sure it would. Yes, they've been notified. But stick to the road. Don't go off into their desert. You see their HQ is positioned on the coastal road." The colonel stretched out his hand. "Well, that's about it, Hard. I'd like to wish you good-luck."

Hard took the hand and replied, "Thank you very much, sir. You've been a great help." He ducked instinctively as a shell exploded a hundred yards away, showering the waiting vehicles with sand. "But what about coming with us, sir? I don't think anyone can do much good here now, sir."

"Thank you for the offer, my boy. But I've already said, I've done enough running. Two years we've been at it now – the old Benghazi Handicap. Up the desert, down the desert. I'm a bit sick of it all. No, I'll stay this time."

Hard clicked to attention and raised his hand to his battered cap in salute. "Best of luck to you, sir."

Wearily the colonel touched his helmet with his swagger stick. "Thank you, Hard. Now you'd better be off with you." He turned and began to trudge away through the sand until he disappeared into the darkness. Instinctively Hard knew he'd never see him again. The one-eyed colonel would die in Tobruk.

He dismissed him. He had to look after his own people now and he knew he didn't have much time left. "All right, drivers," he yelled above the racket, "start them up!" He called to Sergeant Williams. "Sarge, you look after Professor Challenger and Dr Stein in the second truck." He nodded knowingly.

Williams frowned. He didn't like the task that Hard had given him one bit. He had killed enough of the enemy in

136

these last three years, but the thought of killing two of his own in cold blood was utterly repulsive to him. All the same, he put an enthusiasm he did not feel into his voice, knowing that the officer needed all the support he could get. "Will do, sir. Leave it to me."

The Dodge's and the three ton truck's motors burst into noisy life. Hard took one last look at the centre of ruined Tobruk, outlined a dull scarlet by the fires raging at the dock and shook his head. What a waste war was, he told himself, then doubled across to the Dodge and swung himself into the seat next to Guardsman Smith who was driving. "All right, Smithie, take her away."

"Yessir," Smith snapped with that same precise bark he would have given to an officer in peacetime outside Buckingham Palace. Sometimes Hard thought it was a bit of a joke on Smith's part, but at the moment, he hadn't time to concentrate on the matter. He wanted to get them out of Tobruk as soon as possible. For it was quite clear from the intensity of the German barrage, which had gone on all day now, that it wouldn't be long before Rommel and his Afrika Korps attacked.

At a steady 30mph they started heading down the Via Balbia driving eastwards. A lot of traffic was coming from the other direction, ambulances carrying wounded men, their lights on and their bells jingling, trucks towing guns to safer positions and others packed with men who had thrown away their weapons and were deserting even before the attack had started.

Hard looked glum. He didn't like British soldiers to run away, though he had seen plenty of them do so before. At Dunkirk, he had kept men in the dugouts by threatening to shoot anyone who did a bunk. Still it hurt to see it as a regular soldier. At his side, Smith

137

sneered. "A lot of frigging creampuffs. Bomb-happy the lot of them, frightened by a bit of shelling."

Hard forgot the cowards and concentrated on the road. Shells were dropping on both sides of it, but he knew the German gunners wouldn't aim directly at the road. They'd want to use it themselves later and he guessed this might be the direction from which the attack might well come in.

"Smithie floor it," he commanded, telling himself that time was running out for them. They'd have to be out of Tobruk before dawn, if they were going to have a chance. "Anyone gets in your way, run him down," he added harshly.

"Righto, sir," Smith chortled happily, "I wouldn't mind running down some of the cowardly shits. Anyone who runs away from his mates in the line deserves to get the frigging chop." He put his foot down hard. The Dodge surged forward. Behind him Smits increased his speed too . . .

Two miles away, the captured British truck laden with his Brandenburgers was being led towards the Gurkhas' lines by von Almaszy in his captured jeep. He wore a British major's cap, but the rest of his uniform, khaki shirt and shorts, was German. He was not going to run the risk of being found in British uniform and shot as a spy, not even for Rommel. His men were similarly clad.

His aim was to pass through the Gurkha line between two of their weapon pits. In the moonlight he hoped the Gurkhas would take them for British soldiers retreating into the perimeter. Soon Smits would contact his own radioman, sitting behind him in the jeep, and inform where Hard and his gangsters were. He allowed himself a wintry smile, confident that everything was going well . . .

It was just after they had passed the headquarters of the 11th Infantry Brigade to which the Gurkhas belonged that Hard noticed they were being followed. He frowned. That is strange, he told himself puzzled. Everyone else except us is heading away from the front. Why should the lone figure on a motorbike be heading for it?

Carefully he started to study the dark figure on the motorbike, riding some twenty yards or so behind the three ton truck, maintaining the same speed as the little convoy.

Suddenly, on impulse, he said, "Smithie, as soon as the road clears up a bit, do a U-turn and drive back a bit until I tell you to stop."

"What, sir?" Smith exclaimed startled.

Hard repeated his instruction.

Smith nodded. "Okay, sir. There's a gap coming up as it is. At least I can't see any headlights on the opposite side."

"Right. Do it there." Hard opened his pistol holster and eased out his big Colt, taking off the safety catch as he did so.

"Here we go, sir!" Smith yelled and swung the wheel round hard. Next moment they were slewing round in a screech of protesting rubber and the Dodge was ploughing through the sand on the opposite side. The manoeuvre caught Smits completely by surprise. He hit the brake. Too late! The Dodge was already parallel with him and as it came to a halt in a flurry of sand, Hard was leaning out of the offside window, pistol in his hand, yelling, "Hold it there! Get off that bike and come over here – *quick*! And no funny business."

As Dickie Bird, driving the three-tonner braked to a surprised halt and Sergeant Williams yelled, "Anything wrong, sir?" a miserable Smits got off his bike and trudged over to a waiting Hard.

"Take off those goggles," Hard commanded.

Reluctantly he did so, as one of the team dropped over the tailgate and ran to the abandoned bike. He began to search it for weapons.

"Dr Smits!" Challenger yelled from the three tonner, as Smits' face was lit up by a sudden explosion.

"Do you know him, Professor?" Hard cried over the racket.

"Yes, bumped into him several times while we were in Tobruk. I think he's a medical officer with the South Africans."

"Well, why isn't he at his dressing station and why is he following us like this?"

Before anyone had a chance to answer that overwhelming question, the man searching a bike yelled, "Sir, there's a Jerry Schmeisser in the saddlebag – and a radio as well. It's Jerry too. I've seen 'em before in wrecked Jerry vehicles."

"So that's the game, eh!" Hard exploded. "A spy."

Smits quailed. "No," he muttered as if to himself, "I'm— "

"*Sind Sie Deutscher*?" Lisa cried from the truck, speaking that hated language for the first time since 1937.

Hard swung round. "Quick, Dr Stein," he called. "We need to know what this chap is up to."

Lightly she dropped over the tailgate and ran over to where they were standing. She faced Smits, his face frightened and coloured a bright-red hue by the flames of the exploding shells. She remembered that day at

140

Emmerich. She remembered how that monstrous Gestapo man had tortured her. How she had been humiliated, forced to take his evil organ into her mouth and do things which she daren't even think about now in case she cracked up. She faced up to the supposed doctor. "All right, Smits," she cried, "if that's your real name." She pulled the pistol out of her bag and caught all of them by surprise. She levelled the muzzle at his chest, hand as steady as a rock. "Speak before I blow the front of your chest away."

"Good grief," Professor Challenger exclaimed. "Never thought she had the spirit. What an absolutely splendid filly!"

"I . . . I don't— " Smits stammered in English.

*"Halt die blöde Schnauze! Die Wahrheit oder es knallt;"** she rasped hardly in German.

Smits saw how her finger, white-knuckled in the flames, was agitating the trigger of the little pistol. He knew he could expect no mercy from the crazy woman. She was a Jewess, a German Jewess. She'd kill him outright without as much as twitching an eyelid. "I have to follow you." he stuttered.

"Why?" she demanded harshly.

"To report your position."

"To whom?" her questions came like hammer blows.

"To Hauptmann von Almaszy of the Brandenburgers."

"Brandenburgers?" she repeated puzzled.

Hurriedly Hard said, " – a sort of German commandos run by their secret service, the *Abwehr*."

"Ja, ja," a terrified Smits agreed, *"die Abwehr*. But please, please don't shoot me." Smits wrung his hands

* "Hold your stupid trap. Speak or it's going to go off."

together in the classic pose of supplication, the tears now streaming down his cheeks.

"We won't shoot you," Hard called. "If you tell us what we want to know."

"Yes, quick," Lisa urged jerking up the little pistol threateningly, as a fresh salvo of shells burst close by. She knew they had little time left.

"They are to capture you before the offensive starts," Smits quavered. "It was my task to report on you all the time."

"Right then," Hard made a swift decision. "Williams, cover him. I want him to send a radio message to that Brandenburg fellow."

Williams looked at Hard, as if he had suddenly gone mad.

Hard gave him a tight smile. "Don't worry, Sarge. He's going to report us several miles away in the wrong direction." He turned to the trembling agent. "Get to that set. Send this. Target, heading general direction of the British NAAFI. They'll know where that is all right. They've probably already got it targeted for looting . . ."

Five minutes later they were on their way again, leaving Smits standing forlornly next to his smashed bike and radio.

Behind them Tobruk burned.

Book Three

Escape from Tobruk

"Never fear. We shall hold them!"
Professor Challenger to Major Hard, Tobruk,
22 June, 1942

ONE

Christian put the fiver he had borrowed from Quayle into the envelope with the note for Cara and sealed the envelope. He handed it to the handsome staff captain and said, "Thanks for the loan and I'd appreciate it if you'd post this for me. It's to a woman. You can censor it if you like, but really I'm just telling her I'll be back in Malta in a week or so."

Quayle frowned for a moment and at the back of his mind a cynical little voice said, "That's what you think!"

The "Mucky Duck" was about to sail. The dock workers and the Royal Navy men had worked flat out. They had not had time to paint over the new plates so that the scars were still visible but now the old tug was seaworthy again and down on the littered deck, CPO Thirsk was fussing about, getting everything ready for departure.

"What's the latest from the flag office?" Christian asked, smiling a little at Thirsk's antics. It was almost as if he owned the "Mucky Duck" personally.

"The Admiralty signalled at six hundred hours this morning that the German Navy is concentrating its U-boats and E-boats in the general area of Tobruk. Our Intelligence wallahs think that means the Hun offensive is about to start and that their navy is in position to prevent any rescue attempt by our ships at Alex." His frown deepened.

Christian didn't notice it. He had been in danger at sea for so many times now that he accepted danger as a fact of life. He grunted, "And what about the Gib area?"

"Clear apparently," Quayle answered. "The Huns are obviously concentrating all their efforts on Tobruk."

"Hm, that's something to be thankful for." Christian watched as Thirsk tore a strip off Cox, a three badge man of about forty, who had been in the Navy since he was fourteen and had still not qualified for leading seaman's rank, because he was a bit slow and stupid. "What d'yer frigging mean, you was *going* to do it! You *should* have frigging well done it!"

Quayle followed the direction of his gaze and said, "He does take on a bit, doesn't he."

"Well, he and the three striper – Cox – are the only two regulars on board. Old Thirsk gets upset when another regular lets him down. With the hostilities only it doesn't matter so much."

"Hostilities only?" Quayle queried puzzled.

"Yes, chaps who've signed on just for the war."

"I see. What about you, Christian. Are you hostilities only, too?" Quayle asked.

"I suppose, so."

"What will you do, when it's all over?"

Christian shrugged and nodded to the dockies who were now beginning to unwind the hawsers which held them to the quayside. "Don't know. Go back to John Good. From Hull, Hell and Halifax may God preserve us – if they'll have me." He laughed shortly.

146

Again Quayle looked puzzled and Christian enlightened him quickly. "The John Good shipping company sailing from Hull . . . And you, Captain Quayle?"

"After the war? Me, I'll go back to the greasepaint."

"*An actor?*"

Quayle laughed easily. "That's right, skipper." He held out his hand, as down below they started to cast off the hawsers.

"Best of luck. Hope things work out all right for you."

"Thank you."

Hurriedly Quayle clattered down the iron ladder from the bridge and sprang lightly onto the quayside.

Minutes later, the old tug started to nose its way into the Mediterranean, trailing a cloud of black smoke behind it from the great single funnel.

Quayle watched it go, handsome face thoughtful as he peered into the rising sun. He had always thought himself a very rational man – for an actor – but now somehow he felt a sense of foreboding, he didn't quite know why. All the same, he did know that he had seen the last of Lt. Christian. The middle-aged skipper would never go back to Hull. What had Robinson Crusoe said? "Had I the sense to return to Hull, I had been happy." Quayle sucked his teeth. Poor old Christian. Then he turned and got back in the jeep. Slowly the old "Mucky Duck" began to disappear on the horizon . . ."

"Come back, come back, Jolly Jack Straw," Sparks was reading the ballad from a three day old copy of the *Daily Mirror* in his plaintive East Coast voice. "There's ice in the killer sea. Wealther at base closes down for the night. And the ash-blonde WAAF is waiting tea— "

"Put a frigging sock in it," Bunts said, lying on the

opposite bunk, as the "Mucky Duck" ploughed steadily southwards. "What kind of rubbish is that? And hurry up with the *Mirror*. I want to see if Jane's showing her tits again. Last time I saw the *Mirror*, she'd stripped down to her knickers and bra."

Sparks looked at his old comrade contemptuously. "That's all you think about, matey – Beaver. Yer ought to interest yersen a bit more in culture like."

"What do you mean," Bunts retorted. "I know about culture. I won the scripture prize when I was a young'n in Brid. Besides that ain't a real poem. Poems is supposed to rhyme like that one in the head. You know, Sparks. It's no use standing on the seat, the crabs in this place jump six feet." He smiled knowingly. "Now that's real frigging poetry. Come on now hand over the bit with Jane. With a bit o' luck she might have her drawers off as well." He licked his thick lips. "Luvverly grub."

Reluctantly Sparks drew out the sheet with the daily Jane strip cartoon and handed it to Bunts. "What yer gonna do? Have a quiet wank down in the heads, then?"

But the signaller was not fated either to see whether the delightful Jane had her "drawers" down or enjoy a "quiet wank" in the heads. For at that precise moment, the door of the radio shack opened and CPO Thirsk barked, "What a bloody pigsty. Why even a pig'd be ashamed to live in here." He cast a fierce glance around the mess of the little cabin. "I want this little lot cleaned up before the skipper does his first rounds." His voice changed. "You, Sparks, the skipper wants you up on deck." He glared at Bunts. "And you can clean this little lot up in the meantime – and don't frigging well tell me you're not on watch now, cos we're on permanent action stations, the skipper sez."

*   *   *

148

"Sparks," Christian said, holding a big tin mug of tea, well laced with whisky in his hamlike fist, "Our job is to rendezvous with a raiding party on the Libyan. All brown jobs," he meant soldiers. "Now then they're going to establish radio contact with us to let us know where they are before the actual rendezvous." He took a satisfying of the scalding hot mixture and added, "You know about the brown jobs' radio equipment. What kind of a set would they have? And how far does the signal carry."

Sparks thought for a moment. Before them the sea rolled in an endless green swell. Not another ship was in sight. They were all alone in the world. "They'll probably have an 18 set, sir," Sparks replied. "Duff kind of radio. Range is only about a dozen miles, that is on land. Over water might be better. But I wouldn't give it more than 14 or 15 miles. That is to make certain you receive the signal."

"Thanks, Sparks," Christian said his face suddenly thoughtful. "I'll let you have the brown jobs' frequency later when we get closer to the Libyan coast. Off you go."

The young signaller saluted and went out of the bridge-house telling himself that this was probably going to another hairy one if the look on the skipper's face meant anything.

For a minute Christian said nothing. Then he turned to Thirsk, who had taken over the wheel again. "Well, Chiefie, we're going to have to go in pretty close if we're aiming to monitor the brown jobs' progress to the rendezvous. And you know what that means?" He shot the old pretty officer a penetrating look.

"I do, sir. The best way would have come in straight from Med. and picked them up. That way we would have stood less chance of being picked up by their radar— "

"Or surface ships," Christian added quickly.

"That too, sir," Thirsk acknowledged. "Now we'll have to cruise off the enemy coast – for too long."

"Agreed," Christian sucked his teeth. "But there's no other way, I don't think. We'll just have to grin and bear it, I suppose. As soon as it's dark," Christian made a quick decision, "we'll close up for action stations, even if we haven't spotted anything. We'll have to be ready for anything – and everything."

"Ay ay, sir," Thirsk said and peered over the wheel, as if he might spit an enemy craft at any moment.

Half an hour later, it happened. Bunts who was doing a spot of lookout duty aft, cupped his hands up his mouth and yelled up to the bridge, "Sir, we've picked up a shad!"

Christian groaned. "Where?"

Bunts yelled and hastily Christian swung round, tugging up his binoculars as he did so. Yes it was a "shad" or shadow all right. "Blohm and Voss 138, Chiefie," he said to Thirsk.

"Out of range of the Chicago pianos, I suppose, sir?"

"Very definitely, Chiefie. And he'll keep out of range, as you know, until he's whistled up the bombers from Sicily or North Africa. Sod it! Hardly out of Gib and we're up the creek without a ruddy paddle already. Damn!" Angrily Christian let the binoculars fall to his barrel chest.

"Well, sir, it *is* getting dark. You know how quickly the sun goes down in the Med? We might just make then."

Christian shook his head. "No they'll be on to us with the bloody dive-bombers before then. Why we're only

150

about half an hour's flying time from their fields in Sicily. No, they'll catch up with us before darkness falls."

But Christian proved wrong. Night fell and the Germans had still not attacked. Yet as a worried Christian strolled along the deck, encouraging the men at their posts, he could hear that persistent drone in the sky above. The "shad" was still there.

TWO

The night was hideous with the noise of the guns. Tracer streaked back and forth in a deadly morse. Flares soared into the sky on all sides. The preparations for the Desert Fox's great attack were about coming to an end.

In their slit trenches, the faces of the Gurkhas beneath their broad-brimmed jungle hats remained impassive. Most of them were mere boys, recruited straight from their remote hill village, to be sent a thousand miles away to fight in this hot desert. Indeed, Hard thought, as their young British officer briefed him, that some of them didn't look a day older than 12. Yet he knew that when the time came they would fight with a fanaticism unknown to European soldiers. No wonder the Germans feared them.

"All right then," the young captain summed up his instructions, as close by a machine gun began to chatter slowly like an angry woodpecker. "Go through just up the road where my last outposts are. They know you're coming. Then branch off sharply to the left. You'll recognise it. It's marked with empty two gallon petrol cans. We call it the 'Y track'. It leads to the coast and it's our guess that the Germans there are not so thick on the ground. With a bit of luck, Major, you just might— "

He stopped short. The barrage had lifted. Now the

shells were falling to the rear of the waiting Gurkhas' positions. "Christ almighty!" the young office yelled. "They've lifted the shelling on us. *They're coming!*"

Hard knew he was right. The enemy gunners couldn't risk hitting their own men. So they, the German infantry, were already out there, advancing on the Gurkhas.

"Stand to!" the officer yelled and pulled out his revolver. The Gurkhas lifted their weapons. They waited, faces gleaming in the reflected light of the fires. They couldn't hear the Germans advancing: the noise was too tremendous, but they knew they were there. Soon, very soon, the killing would commence.

Hard waited no longer. "Thanks," he yelled and dived into the seat next to Smith at the wheel of the Dodge. "Move it, Smithie."

"Good luck Johnnie Gurkha," Smith cried to the nearest little Gurkha and slammed home first gear. The Dodge lurched forward.

Now the German infantry, clearly recognisable in their coal-scuttle helmets were coming in on both sides of the road. They came in long line, upper bodies bent, as if they were fighting a strong wind, weapons held at the high port. Up front their officers kept turning and waved their pistols to urge them on. Behind, NCOs, with Schmeisser machine pistols clasped across their chests looked warily from side to side, on the lookout for anyone who was lagging behind out of fear or cowardice. Then they would fire.

"Cor ferk a duck!" Smith cursed in awe, as the flashes of gunfire lit up the advancing infantry time and time again. "It looks as if the whole of Hitler's mob is out there."

"Keep your eye on the road," Hard commanded. "We should be turning off soon – and it can't be too soon for me. We won't go undetected for much longer."

Behind them the whole of the Gurkha line had erupted in fire. Rifles snapped, Bren guns chattered, two-inch mortars sang their song of sudden death. Germans were stumbling and falling everywhere. *"Los Manner"*, the officers yelled, as here and there the infantry faltered. *"Weiter . . . immer weiter Los!"*

A little bunch of Gurkhas appeared out of nowhere, Kukris flashing silver in the light of the exploding shells. Fearlessly they launched themselves on the nearest Germans, long knives dealing out death in an instant. They chopped, gouged, slashed until one by one they went down under the German fire.

Hard breathed out hard. What men, he told himself. A white painted petrol can loomed up to the left. Then another. "Y-track, Smithie," he yelled above the wild screams and shrieks of the infantry battle. "Gildy, turn off for Chris sake!"

Smith swung the wheel round.

Hard flashed a look behind him. The truck had done the same, turning off the smooth tarmac of the coastal road onto the bumpy rock and sand of the Y-track. As it did so, a burst of wild tracer followed it, kicking up angry little spurts of sand just behind its rear axle.

"We've been spotted!" Hard yelled.

Crazily Guardsman Smith zig-zagged between the cans along both sides of the Y-track. A lone German loomed up out of the glowing darkness. He had a stick grenade in his raised right hand. Hard fire. He missed. The German threw a grenade and ducked. It hit the Dodge and flew off into the night to land next to the German. It exploded in an ugly spurt of angry-red flame. The German was lifted

154

clean off the ground. When he slammed down again he was minus his head.

Now firing was coming in from both sides. Hard prayed that the engines of the two vehicles wouldn't be hit. That would be the end. In the vehicles the Group were firing back. The night was stabbed time and time again with vicious flame. The glass in front of Hard splintered suddenly into a glittering spider's web. He raised both feet. With both feet held tightly together he rammed them against the windscreen with all his strength. The glass gave and he could feel the sudden blood running down his ankles. But at least he could see once more.

A German halftrack came crawling out from a kind of hut to the left. In the three tonner the gunner swung his twin Brownings round. They chattered furiously. Tracer streamed towards the open half-track. The Germans inside went down in a crazy, confused heap, arms and legs flailing. The driver slumped across the wheel but the halftrack continued to drive towards the sea, as if it intended to bury itself there.

Hard breathed out hard. He knew they had driven into the German supporting flank. It was not as strong as the main attack on the Gurkha positions, but it was the usual German tactic in order to turn the flank of a strongly held position. Now as they jolted and bumped down the Y-Track, he wondered just what its depth was. For their luck couldn't hold out for ever if they had to continue much longer like this. They were being fired at from both sides.

Then they did strike lucky – behind them the Gurkhas, carried away by that wild atavistic lust to kill in battle of theirs, suddenly rose from their weaponpits and slit trenches. Yelling their war cries in Gurkhali, rifles abandoned for their kukris and Tommy guns they surged forward, stumbling and slipping over the bodies of dead Germans. The enemy was caught completely by surprise. Suddenly the Gurkhas were in among them, chopping and slashing. They showed no quarter and expected none. If a German went down, his face was slashed to pieces mercilessly. Even those who cried *"Kamerad"*, threw away their weapons, and raised their hands in surrender, hadn't a chance. With one bold slice the Gurkhas chopped their heads off.

Angrily the Gurkha officers shrilled their whistles, bellowed their orders for the little men to return to their trenches. They had no effect. The Gurkhas, getting ever fewer now, as the German machine guns opened up on them, kept pushing forward, slashing and chopping to left and right.

"What soldiers!" Smith cried above the snap-and-crackle of the bitter small arms fight. "Even yer guards wouldn't have been able to pull anything like that off. Brave little yeller buggers!"

Hard made no reply. He was praying that they were going to make it now, for the firing and shouts were dying away on both sides of the Y-track now. Here and there in the red glowing darkness, he caught glimpses of Germans fleeing back the way they had come, obviously terrified of the little men. Now they had no time for the escapers.

They roared on.

From somewhere there was the grunt bark and rush of air as an anti-tank gun opened up. A solid white blob hurried towards them at a crazy speed. "Christ almigh— " Smith began. He never finished the curse. There was the great hollow boom of metal striking metal. The Dodge came to an abrupt stop. Suddenly the air was full of the stench of escaping petrol, as the Dodge started to sink on a broken front axle.

Hard shook his head, "Bale out everybody!" he cried frantically.

For a moment a shocked Smith at the wheel seemed unable to act. Hard gave him a great push and roared "*Out!*" The Guardsman fell onto the sand.

"*Run!*" Hard roared.

Suddenly they were all running as hard as they could. It was just in time. The ruptured engine went up in a huge hush of flames the next moment. The fire seared the rest of the vehicle like a blow-torch. In the back of the blazing Dodge, the ammunition began to explode, zig-zagging in every direction as behind them the three tonner braked to a stop, coloured in a flash with the reds, greens and whites of the explosions.

"Anybody hurt?" Hard gasped, as he flopped into the sand with rest, feeling the searing heat of the burning truck even at that distance.

"Lofty Long got a bit of shrapnel in his back," someone answered.

Another cried. "Burnt me hands, sir."

Williams jumped down from the back of the three-tonner. "You all right, sir?" he asked urgently.

"I'm all right, Sarge," Hard replied, wiping the sudden sweat from his thin face. "Check out the casualty situation. What a fine bollocks this all is," he added, realising that now there was only the one vehicle and it couldn't possibly accommodate all of them. They would have to slog the rest of the way on foot and that meant they'd have to go at the pace of the slowest of the team. He rose slowly to his feet.

The firing in the area of the Gurkha lines had begun

to die way and he reasoned that the little men's positions had been overrun. Indeed now he could hear the faint rattle of tank tracks. He knew what that meant. Rommel was sending in his armour, which at night he always used with a screen of infantry. He frowned. What was left of the Gurkhas wouldn't stand a chance against the Desert Fox's panzers, that was for sure.

Challenger clambered out of the three tonner and looked at the tall private whose shirt back was ripped and bloody from the shrapnel wound. "That poor chap can have my place in the truck," he boomed.

"Come off it, Dad," Lofty Long chortled. "I'm half your age, even if I've got a bit o' tin in me back, I can make it on foot."

Challenger eyed him angrily. "Dad indeed," he barked. "Now get in that truck at once, do you hear. And give me that rifle too." He grabbed the soldier's Lee Enfield.

"But you're a civvie. They'll shoot you if they catch you with a civvie."

Challenger was unmoved by the danger. "What do you think they'll do to me, if they catch me anyway?" he commented.

Inside the truck Lisa shivered as she reached out her hand to help the wounded man into the vehicle.

"All right," Hard yelled above the noise. "No more time to waste. Move off Dickie Bird. The rest of us will hoof it."

As the truck started to move again in low gear, the rest of them shouldered their weapons, knowing it was going to be a long walk; and tomorrow they'd be right smackup in the middle of the Afrika Korps positions. As Smith expressed it with a weary sigh, "It's gonna be roses, frigging roses all the way . . ."

THREE

Hauptmann von Almaszy fumed, quite unconcerned about the potential danger he and his small group of Brandenburgers were in. Over at the NAAFI, drunken South African soldiers, all discipline vanished, were looting the place. Others were staggering to the burning docks, crying in Afrikaans and English, "Let's get a boat . . . Got to have a boat!" It was clear that the South African Division was about finished, for ever more and more soldiers, most of them without arms, were streaming into the centre of Tobruk. But in all the confusion and chaos, there was no sign of Hard and his killers. And where was Smits, who had said they would be at this place?

A little helplessly von Almaszy wondered what he should do? Should he retreat before someone started asking awkward questions? Or should he attempt to find Smits to find out what had gone wrong?

Over at the NAAFI, where South Africans were tossing crates of beer through the smashed upper windows to their cheering mates below, a drunken giant had got a black man by the throat and was smashing his other fist into the terrified black's face crying in Afrikaans, "It's all your fault, you damn nigger Kaffir . . . It's all your fault!"

Von Almaszy shook his head in disgust. How brutal the English and their white allies were to the natives of their Empire! It was a wonder, he told himself, that they had retained it so long. Indeed, he supposed, that was the way they kept the natives tame – by sheer brutality.

Over at the harbour a fresh squadron of Stuka dive-bombers were falling out of the dawn sky, shrieking down, sirens screaming, evil little black eggs tumbling from their bellies, while the drunken South Africans fled shrieking.

Von Almaszy decided it would serve no purpose for him to remain here any longer. The English had disappeared, and he was certain he would not find them here in the centre of this awful mess. It was just then that Dietz, his radioman, doubled across. He looked to left and right to check if he might be overheard and said, "*Herr Hauptmann—* "

"Speak English," von Almaszy interrupted him sharply.

"Yessir," Dietz said. "A radio message. Air Force reports they have found the tug . . . *Your* tug."

Von Almaszy's wizened old face lit up. "What?"

Dietz repeated the information.

Von Almaszy whistled softly. "Then we've got them again," he said to himself. "The tug will lead us to them, after all." His voice heightened. "Signal HQ to keep contact with tug and keep us informed at all times. Now let's get out of this madhouse."

"Hey you!" a harsh voice yelled just as they were about to return to the captured jeep, "what are you doing here? Why aren't you back in the line?"

Von Almaszy and the radioman turned startled.

A big burly captain of military police stood there, flanked by two other redcaps, both carrying sten guns.

"You're British, aren't you," he nodded to the insignia

of the British 50th Infantry Division on the mudguards of the jeep. "Tyne-Tees, isn't it? And the British aren't abandoning their positions like this Springbok rabble." He looked hard at von Almaszy, "Well, what have you to say for yourself, Captain?"

Von Almaszy's cunning old brain raced. He knew he spoke fluent English, but with an accent. The MP officer was obviously no fool. He'd pick up the accent immediately. He made his decision. Out of the corner of his mouth, he said to Dietz, who was slightly behind him. "Use me as cover and shoot. Then run like hell."

Over the port one of the Stukas had been hit by anti-aircraft fire. Now it was falling out of the sky, trailing thick black smoke behind to the drunken cheers of the South Africans. For a moment the MP officer's attention was distracted by the cheering. He turned slightly. It was the moment of inattention that Dietz needed. He pulled out his silenced pistol. There was a soft plop. The MP officer gave a sudden groan. He looked down at the patch of blood on his immaculate shirt, as if greatly surprised. Suddenly his knees began to give way beneath him like those of a newly born foal.

"*Run!*" von Almaszy yelled in German

Then the two of them were pelting back to the jeep, arms working back and forth like pistons, while the two MPs finally reacted and started fumbling to unsling their sten guns. An instant later, as the driver slewed the jeep round in a great flurry of dust, they opened fire. Slugs cut the air all around the jeep and the captured Bedford truck. Wild firing broke out on all sides, as the two vehicles barrelled down the road, their drivers hunched over their wheels, going all out. They were escaping, von Almaszy knew that, but soon they would have to abandon the

161

vehicles with their insignia of the British 50th Infantry Division. They'd stand out like a sore thumb now. *"Great crap on the Christmas tree,"* he cursed angrily to himself, as they sped away, things are going badly wrong . . .

Some fifty miles away off the coast of Libya that dawn, Christian felt the same. The "shad", although it was naturally a different plane, was still with them, droning monotonously through the dawn sky, keeping the "Mucky Duck" under constant surveillance. It angered Christian. They were damnably impotent. He strode along the deck to the "monkey island" where the tug's twin Oerlikons were located. He said to the new gunner from the coastal artillery, a "brown job", but a decent young corporal with a pleasant open face, "What do you think, Corporal? Any chance of knocking the sod out of the sky?"

The Corporal clicked to attention as if he were still back in Gibraltar. "It'd be a real fluke, sir. I'm afraid, sir, that he's a good five hundred yards out of range. And those Fockes are a tough plane." He slapped the breech of the Oerlikon. "Even if I could hit him, I have a feeling that the Oerlikon's 20mm shells wouldn't knock him out of the sky."

Christian nodded his understanding. "Ah, well," he said, "keep your eyes on the damn thing. You never know, we might get lucky yet, Corporal."

"Yessir. Will do so, sir."

Gloomily Christian moved on, as the Corporal returned to polishing the breech of his guns as if his life depended upon it. He walked over to Bunts who was leaning over the rail, having a "quiet spit-and-a-draw", as he phrased it.

He made some pretence of coming to attention, but Christian stopped him with a somewhat weary wave of his hand. "All right, Bunts, you're no brown job. I won't have you hurting yerself playing soldier. Carry on with your filthy weed."

"Thank you, sir." Bunts took another draw at the cigarette which he had cupped in his hand to protect it from the wind, sailor-fashion. "Gets right on my tits, sir, that shad does," he said.

Christian looked up at the tiny shape high in the sky above them, "It doesn't do much for me either," he said gloomily. "Damned thing."

Bunts smiled. "Did you ever hear the one about the Fleet Air bloke who went to get a gong from King George?"

"No," Christian answered without too much interest.

"Well, sir, the old King, who as you know, stutters badly, asked the pilot. 'Did . . . didn't you shoot down a Focke-Wulf to get this?' And pilot said. 'No, sir, it was *two* Focke-Wulfs.' And the King, he sez, 'Never mind, you're only gonna g . . . g . . . get one f-f-focking medal.'" Bunts laughed heartily at his own joke and Christian said, "That one's so old that it's got grey hair."

"Just trying to cheer you up, sir," Bunts said as Christian moved on, still followed by the insidiously maddening drone of the "shad".

Half an hour later Sparks came up to the bridge with the first signal from Hard and his party. "Sorry I'm a bit slow," Sparks said, the message form held inside his cap in traditional naval fashion. "But the signal was faint and I had a bit of trouble decoding."

"All right, Sparks. Thank you. Get back to the job."

Swiftly Christian read the message and passed it to Thirsk to read, but the latter said, "Tell me what it says, sir, please. I've left my specs down below."

"A sailor with specs!" Christian snorted in mock disgust. "Whoever heard of such like. You *really* must have served with Nelson at Trafalgar. In short, Hard has moved out of Tobruk safely. Running into some trouble. But he's now proceeding in a north-westerly direction heading for the pick-up point."

It was then that Thirsk sprang his bombshell. "Sir, it's just come to me!" he cried in sudden alarm.

"What, Chiefie?" Christian rapped, catching the note of urgent alarm in the old petty officer's voice.

"That shad, sir."

"What about it?"

Thirsk took his eyes off the instruments and looked at him, his face suddenly white and drawn and looking very old. "That shad hasn't whistled up the dive bombers to attack us, because it doesn't want us sunk."

"What the devil do you mean, Chiefie?"

"This, sir. That shad's following us because he knows we will lead him right to Major Hard's party and the two civvies."

"Oh Christ Chiefie!" Christian cried aghast. "You're right! It can be the only reason why they're still shadowing us and we haven't been bloody attacked." Christian felt a great anger well up inside of him. It was so bloody unfair. He couldn't just abandon Hard and his chaps. But once the "Mucky Duck" had led the Jerries to the rendezvous, both Hard's party and the crew of the "Mucky Duck" would get the chop. Everything would be for nothing.

"What are you going to do, sir?" Thirsk, equally alarmed, for he had just come to the same conclusion as Christian had. "We can let the brown jobs down of course. But what will happen to our own matelots when . . ." His voice trailed away to nothing, as if he didn't want to think that particular thought to its dreadful end.

Christian's mind raced, as he looked up again at the sky. There the bastard was, black dot in the bright blue wash of the sky; and as before the bastard was keeping obstinately out of range.

Thirsk looked at him expectantly.

Christian sucked his teeth and wished longingly for a stiff, a very stiff, drink. But he knew that there was no time for that now. He had to think. He had to get rid of the "shad" by nightfall, for he guessed Hard would want the pickup from the coast during the hours of darkness. It would be safer that way. "You see, Chiefie," he said slowly, eyes remote, as the vague idea started to uncurl in his mind, "we've got to lure the sod down. I mean low enough to give ourselves a chance to knock the swine out of the sky."

Chief Petty Officer Thirsk nodded his grizzled head. "I know, sir. But how we're gonna to do it – that's the question."

"Look Chiefie," now it was Christian's turn to ask the questions, "how much heat do you think the forrard deck would stand?"

Thirsk was puzzled, but he answered all the same. "Well, as you know, sir, it's thin steel plate, but there is caulking – and there's wood underneath. That's the way they built them in the twenties. My guess is that the deck would stand a fair amount of heat, but not too much." He waited, the puzzled look on his wrinkled face.

Christian grinned, a rare event with him. "Chiefie," he said, "I think we're going to have an engine room fire . . ."

FOUR

Dickie Bird groaned and got up holding his back.

"Well?" Hard demanded, as the driver wiped the sweat of his oil-blackened face.

"I've plugged the radiator – chewing gum and sand. And I've got a spark."

"Excellent," Hard breathed out a sigh of relief. The engine of the three tonner had been hit by a burst of enemy machine gunfire an hour before. The truck, with everyone hanging on the best they could, ran for another ten minutes until they had managed to get away safely and then the holed radiator had run empty and they had been forced to stop. Thus it was that for the last thirty minutes Dickie Bird had worked feverishly on the engine to get it ready to move again.

"We still got petrol and there's enough oil in the sump," Dickie Bird continued, "so that she won't seize up for another thirty miles or so and if we can all sacrifice a pint of water from our water bottles— "

"We can."

"Then we can fill up the radiator again. But there's one catch, sir."

"What's that?" Hard asked hurriedly. In an hour it would be dark and by then he wanted to have a perimeter established at the natural harbour, ready for

166

the rendezvous with the *Black Swan*.

"The battery's about as dead as a doornail," Dickie Bird pointed a grease-stained finger at the rise ahead of them. "But if we could get the sod up there. There's downhill slope enough, I'm certain, to get her started before we hit the desert floor again."

Hard whistled softly. "It looks like tough titty to me," he said slowly. "The truck's damn heavy— " He didn't finish and Dickie Bird said with a note of finality in his voice, "We can but try, sir."

Hard knew he was right. The men had had about enough. As long as they could take it in turns to have a ride on the truck, he'd get them to the rendezvous. If they didn't, then he'd just have to find a hide-out and let them rest up for a while. That was something he didn't think was very wise at this moment in time.

Hurriedly they set to work, as behind them some miles away the attack on Tobruk came to its climax. That fact lent speed to their actions, for all of them knew that once Rommel had captured the vital British supply base, he would start heading in their direction to launch his attack on Egypt. Swiftly the radiator was filled up from their waterbottles. Then they set to work to flatten a path up the slope. The harder and firmer the sand of the path the less hard work it would be for them later when they attempted to push the heavy truck up it. Others ripped out all the fittings from the Bedford, anything that would make it lighter, even its spare wheel. Half an hour later they were lathered in sweat, even Lisa, whose breasts bulged through the sweat-blackened sticky material of her khaki shirt. But now they were ready.

Hard wiped away the sweat which dripped from his eyebrows as if from a leaky tap and gasped, "All right,

Dickie. It's your idea. You'll have the honour of driving the bastard."

"Better than pushing, sir," Bird said cheekily. He got in behind the wheel and yelped with pain as he felt the burning hot metal. He thrust home neutral and let the brake off. "Ready, sir," he called. He smiled but all of them could see the tension in his lean, tanned face. They knew why. This was the last chance they might have. If the truck didn't start, it wouldn't be long before the Germans captured them and they all knew what their fate would be then.

They took the strain, even Lisa. The wheels squeaked. Nothing happened. "Once again!" Hard yelled and pressed his shoulder hard against the big truck. All of them bent and heaved with all their strength, the veins standing out at their temples with the strain. The truck creaked. Suddenly it started to move.

"Come on, chaps!" Challenger bellowed, his face lathered in sweat as if it had been greased. "Put some back into it!"

Now the back-breaking job of pushing the truck up the incline commenced. Under that murderous sun, they edged it up inch by inch, their breath coming in great gasping sobs. Hard felt the veins in his temples hammering away madly as if they might break their way out at any moment. His shoulder muscles felt as if red hot pokers were being thrust into them. Behind him Smith slipped and almost lost his grip. Desperately he grabbed a stanchion and yelped with pain as it pulled off two of his fingernails. Still he pushed on.

Time seemed to pass with leaden feet. Their whole world consisted of that blinding, murderously hot sun, their sweat-soaked uniforms and that back-breaking grind of heaving, shoving, panting, which seemed to go on for ever.

Finally after what appeared an eternity, they reached the summit to collapse there in the sand exhausted, heaving and gasping like a school of stranded whales.

Hard gave them five minutes before gasping in a voice he hardly recognised as his own, "All right, one last effort lads. Let's get the bastard started . . . Excuse my French, Dr Stein."

She gave him a weary grin, "Don't apologise, Major. It *is* a real bastard."

"I say, old girl," Challenger began then thought better of it and stopped.

There were protests and groans. But one by one the exhausted men staggered to their feet. They stood there, swaying from side to side like drunks. Hard moved to the truck, seeing nothing but the blue waves of the heat shimmering and trembling above the sand.

"Once more into the breach, dear friends," Challenger boomed and was the first to apply his massive shoulder to the side of the truck, One by one the others followed. Hard wet his tongue which seemed three times its normal size and commanded, *"Now!"*

Bird crashed home second gear and took off the hand brake. Slowly, painfully, the heavy truck breasted the rise. It began to limber forward, gathering speed now. They broke into a clumsy trot. The pressure and strain were easing off. One by one they let go or lost contact, falling to their knees in the sand, staring after the truck.

Now Dickie Bird was on his own. Still he did not lift his foot from the depressed clutch. He knew desperately that he had only one chance. A boulder boomed up out of the sand directly in his path.

Behind him still on his knees, Hard gasped, "Miss it . . . for crissake, miss it!"

Bird swerved and sailed by the boulder. Still he kept the clutch depressed, eyes bulging out of his head like those of a man demented as he calculated how many yards he had left before he hit the flat sand plain below.

"*Now!*" he commanded himself, giving vent to all his tension in a great angry roar. He eased his foot off the clutch and pressed the accelerator. Behind him Hard pressed his hands together. "Come on, Dickie," he roared, "get the bastard to start!"

Nothing happened!

Lisa Stein sobbed, "Please start . . . please."

Abruptly the truck heaved violently. Thick black smoke shot from its exhaust. Hard stopped breathing. Was this it? Still nothing happened. At the wheel Dickie Bird cursed and cursed. He had only about twenty yards left before he hit the flat stretch. It was now or never.

Suddenly there was a long low keening. It was like some eerie Highland dirge played on the pipes. Hard's eyes widened. More and more smoke was pouring from the exhaust. And now Dickie Bird had only about ten yards left. The noise grew ever louder. It sounded to Hard as if the Bedford might blow up at any moment. There was a series of sharp bursts of backfire. Five yards left! A burst of white smoke. A violent sparking. Suddenly there was a tremendous burst of engine noise. The truck shot forward. Moments later it was on the flat with a sobbing, sweat-soaked Dickie Bird gunning the engine desperately for all it was worth. He had done it . . . *he had done it*!

Crying madly, waving their arms like crazy people, their exhaustion forgotten for a while, they stumbled and ran down the slope to where a sweating, limp Dickie Bird was still gunning the engine of the truck – and grinning like an idiot.

"Good work, Dickie," Hard croaked and the others cried their approval.

Suddenly, however, the big grin disappeared from Bird's sweat-lathered face to be replaced by a look of alarm.

"What is it?" Hard rasped.

"Over yonder, sir. Look." With an anxious nod of his head, Dickie Bird indicated to their right. "At three o'clock, sir."

Hard flashed a glance in that direction. Silhouetted starkly against the yellow-red glare of the afternoon sun, three riders sat motionless on their camels some 500 yards away staring at the truck and the little party of sweat-lathered soldiers. "Damn," he exclaimed, "not that – *now!*"

"What's the matter?" Challenger asked. "They're only Arabs, aren't they?"

"Yes," Hard answered. "Senussi, they'd sell their own mothers to the Huns," he added bitterly.

"But why, I thought they hated the Italians who beat them in battle in the twenties and early thirties," Challenger objected.

"They probably do," Hard answered, as Williams unslung his rifle hastily. "But they think the Germans are going to give them their freedom. Besides the Germans always give them money."

"For what?" Challenger asked puzzled.

"For us, or any Briton who happens to be defenceless and can be taken," Hard said harshly. Next to him Williams took aim. "They won't attempt to take us themselves this time. There are too many of us and we're armed. But you bet your life if we don't— "

Crack! Williams fired. The closest of the three Arabs flung up his arms, as if he were climbing the rungs of an invisible ladder. Next moment he slithered from his camel and flopped into the sand. Thereafter he didn't move.

Rapidly Williams fired off the whole magazine. But now the Arabs had been warned. They struck their animals with their goads. Next moment they had jerked the camels round and were racing away across the desert at a great rate.

"Sod it!" Williams cursed, ejecting the last cartridge case from the smoking chamber of his rifle. "Sorry I missed the two others, sir."

"No matter," Hard said, "we'd better get moving. Those Arabs have got an uncanny sense of where people are in the desert. God knows how, but they can always find people in the most trackless type of terrain. They'll soon sniff out the Germans nearest to us and lead them to us so that they can get their blood money. So we must move at speed. We'll change places in the truck every fifteen minutes. But we've got to keep up the pace." He looked very worried. "Now – *move*!"

They moved.

FIVE

"*Holy strawsack,*" the second pilot of the Focke exclaimed, "*the Tommy's on fire!*"

"What?" the chief pilot cried. He peered down through gleaming perspex of the canopy at the sea far below. In it the tiny speck of a ship now had a cherry-red flame burning on its foredeck. "*Himmelherrje,*" he gasped, "you're shitting well eight, Dieter."

"The engine room might have gone up," the other pilot suggested. "You can see she's stopping. What do you think – what shall we do?"

The chief pilot pulled a wry face. He knew just how important the tug they were shadowing was. Apparently if he lost her, an important operation would be aborted. "Remember *Herr Major,*" the CO had told him at the briefing. "This matter had been apparently decided at the highest level. Don't let me or the squadron down." The chief pilot made up his mind. "Get the radio man to radio base what is happening down there. In the meantime I think we'll go down and have a look-see at how serious that fire is."

As the second pilot stumbled down narrow fuselage to carry out his orders, the chief pilot pressed the wheel forward. The plane's nose sank and it started to descend. They were on their way.

Down below, Christian whistled softly. "They've bought it, Chiefie," he exclaimed.

Thirsk's face, sweat-glazed with the heat of the petrol fire, now raging below on the foredeck, lit up. "Thank God, Sir!" he cried above the crackle of the flames which had almost reached as high as the bridge. "Everybody's standing by. But he'd better get down sharpish. We can't let that fire go on much longer. The deck's going to give in another couple of minutes, sir."

Christian nodded urgently. Every man was on alert now, including those he had managed to lever out of the engine room. Every gun was manned and on the firedeck, the fire teams were standing with their hoses, ready to go into action immediately he gave the signal. "Start praying, Chiefie," he said and darted out of the bridgehouse. "We need every little bit of help we can get . . ."

The co-pilot said, "Base has radioed that you have to keep up the surveillance. You can investigate the fire now . . . Oh, yes, and they're scrambling the fighters at Catania now."

The chief pilot nodded his helmeted head, as he concentrated on bringing the big four-engined plane down. "Are the gunners alerted?" he rasped.

"Yes."

"Tell 'em to keep their eyes peeled. The Tommies are cunning bastards."

"Like tinned tomatoes," the younger man replied cheerfully, glad of a bit of action after the long boring routine of shadowing the English tug.

"Here we go then," the chief pilot snapped . . .

"One thousand feet, sir," the "brown job" at the twin Oerlikon sang out gleefully, not taking his gaze off the big plane for a moment. "Brother, am I going to enjoy this!"

Below him the rating manning the PAC rockets, which flung up wire hawsers to entangle in low-flying planes engines and props, shouted, "Let's get the bugger low enough first. He's a cagey one. He's levelling off— "

"But he's in range," the brown job cried back. "Now what about trying this one on for size, *arsehole*?" He pressed the trigger. A stream of white tracer shells zipped upwards. Down below the rating fired his rockets. In an instant the whole length of the "Mucky Duck" erupted into angry firing. Some of the crew were even blazing away with the Tommy guns that Christian had pleaded for in Gibraltar.

Great metal chunks started to rain down from the enemy plane. But the pilot continued to keep on flying, dragging the plane's evil black shadow behind it across the surface of the sea.

"Come on . . . come on!" Christian yelled to himself in frenzied anticipation, digging the nails of one hand cruelly into the palm of the other. "Fall out of the sodding sky, won't you!"

At the controls, the chief pilot cried, "The cunning English. That damned Tommy is not on fire really. They've shitting well tricked us!" He grabbed the controls and started to heave them back with all his strength, as the fuselage filled with the acrid stench of spent ammunition and down below the enemy blazed away furiously so that he seemed to be flying through a white net of shells and slugs. Behind, the tailend gunner blazed away furiously, trying to knock out the English gunners with his own twin cannon.

Suddenly there was a sharp crack. The perspex in front of the pilot splintered. A whiff of evil yellow smoke rushed in through the gap. Momentarily the pilot was blinded. But besides him the co-pilot grabbed the controls and continued to heave them back, his eyes bulging from their sockets with the effort.

"*Schnell, Dieter. Schnell, Mensch*! Get her up!" the pilot yelled above the roar of the wind howling through the holed canopy now.

"The sow's not answering," the other yelled back. "I'm getting no shitting power!"

"They must . . . *must*!" the other man shrieked in a sudden frenzy of fear. He grabbed his own controls and, bracing his feet against the fuselage, heaved. Nothing happened. *The plane was out of control.*

"We're heading for the drink," Dieter yelled. "We're going to have to ditch her."

"No!" the other man roared back. "The Tommies'd murder us. I know them of old." He redoubled his efforts, his face purple with strain and fury.

But now the plane was definitely coming down, the controls jammed by the brown job's shells for good. The two pilots gave up. The chief pilot pressed his throat mike hastily. "Prepare to bale out – everyone!" He ripped the wires away and fumbled behind his seat for his parachute. Next to him, the co-pilot, his blue eyes wild with fear, did the same.

Suddenly, startlingly, the plane staggered as if it had just run into a brick wall. The engines cut out. Abruptly there was a great howling silence and rush of wind as the Focke Wulfe fell out of the sky. They were heading for the water . . .

"*Hurrah*!" a great, happy cheer went up from the crew of the "Mucky Duck". "*Hurrah*!" Sweat-lathered, exhausted, but happy the gunners slumped across their smoking weapons as the four-engined "shad" went into its dive of death, thick black smoke trailing behind it as it did so. They felt no pity for the enemy trapped inside it heading for a watery grave, just relief that they, themselves, had been saved. A moment or two later the "shad" hit the surface of the Mediterranean and in a great splash went under. There was a series of ripples spreading ever outwards, tinged with oil. A few obscene belches of escaping air followed with odd bits of equipment bobbing up and down on the agitated surface of the water. Then gradually it calmed. None of the crew appeared for which Christian was grateful. He wouldn't have attempted to rescue them, for like all wartime sailors he hated the "shads" more than he did the enemy divebombers.

He left the fire-fighting party and wiping the sweat from his brow, he strode to the money island where the Oerlikons were. For he guessed it had been the young brown job who had brought the German down with his twin cannon. He told himself that the open-faced young artillery corporal deserved a pat on the back.

But the brown job was no longer open-faced. A burst of German machine-gun fire had ripped away his features, which were melting down his chest like red wax. Now he lay hanging over the guns, dead, the only sound coming from him the steady drip-drip of his blood falling to the pool on the deck below. Next to him the rating who had manned the rockets was sobbing and wringing his hands like a broken-hearted mother.

"It's all right, son," Christian said in a surprisingly soft voice for him, soothingly. "I'll see to the poor chap. You just go down to the galley and scrounge yourself a cup of char."

"Thank you, sir," the rating said thickly.

"And send Adam the sailmaker up when you do," Christian called after him.

Five minutes later the two of them, the skipper and the wizened sailmaker, who had been called up as a reservist, were sewing the body up in a piece of sailcloth. Before they reached the face, however, the old three-striper took his curved steel needle and made the traditional "last stitch".

Christian winced involuntarily as the old sailmaker thrust his needle through the dead man's bloody nose. The tradition was that only in this way he could satisfy himself that the body he was stitching for burial at sea was really dead.

Adam grunted something and then he completed sewing up the canvas, saying, as if this were something he did every day, "He's ready, sir."

"Thank you," Christian said and beckoned to a couple of ratings watching to come and carry the body. "And you," he called to a third sailor, "go and fetch the ensign. The lad ought to have a decent burial for what he did."

Five minutes later those who were still not damping down the fire assembled on the aft deck, where the corpse under the ensign was balanced by a couple of solemn ratings. Christian took off his battered white cap, with brass insignia already green from a lack of polishing. "We've only known him for a couple of days. In fact," he added awkwardly, "I didn't even find out his name. So there's not much I can say about him, shipmates, save that he was a brave lad who helped to save our bacon. I'm not going to say a prayer, because I don't know how. All I'm going to say is, God bless him and look after him, like I hope he'll look after all of us." He nodded grimly to the two ratings at the rail.

Holding the ensign with one hand, each used the other to shove the canvas bundle over the side. It slid over the rail and disappeared into the darkening water with a splash.

"Caps on!" CPO Thirsk barked. He saluted Christian, "Permission to dismiss the men, sir?"

"Yes, carry on," Christian said softly, returning the salute absent-mindedly, as if his thoughts were elsewhere.

The ratings went back to their duties, including Thirsk after he had given Christian a long hard searching look. Now Christian was alone on this part of the deck, staring at the sinking sun to the west. In an hour it would be pitch-black and then they'd go in. On the morrow it would be all over and he'd be glad. He rubbed his hand wearily across his forehead. He told himself he was getting too tired, too old for this bloody business. What he needed now was a shore job, something simple in stores, say, with his whisky and Cara and a warm bed at night. He pulled a wry face. The war had about done him.

It was then that sparks came running down the deck, crying, "Sir, sir . . . I had contact . . . They signalled they were going to rendezvous this night . . . *and then their set went dead on me . . .*"

SIX

They had been bending over the fresh steaming camel turds when it had happened. Guardsman Smith, who had been out in the Western Desert since 1939 and was their expert, had been pulling one of the turds apart with his bayonet. "If it's barley, you find," he had been lecturing them, "then we gave the Wogs the fodder. Then they'll be probably friendlies. If it's maize, then they won't, cos they get the maize as fodder from the Eyeties."

They had waited anxiously (though Hard personally had been slightly amused by Smith's pedantic manner), for the Guardsman's findings.

"Maize," he said finally, pointing at the grains in the steaming turd. "So the Eyeties provided the fodder." And you can take it it's them sodding Sen— "

The crackle of fire had broken into his little lecture as the first slugs had slammed into the side of the Bedford truck.

They had dropped to the ground automatically and had begun returning the fire, though the Arabs who had shot at them had retreated instantly over the slope of the closest dune. But only for a few moments. Hard had yelled, "Cease firing. Save your ammo. Let's get moving again. The Wogs wouldn't have attacked without knowing that the Jerries are coming up. Move it!"

They had.

Now the truck, its canvas ripped and torn by the Arab fire, moved slowly across the face of the coastal plain, with those who were walking sheltering on the far side. Up next to the steaming, overheated motor, which was emitting threatening noises all the time, as if it could seize up at any minute, Hard stared almost longingly to his front hoping to catch the first glimpse of the sea. But the horizon remained stubbornly yellow, the yellow of the desert.

"Here they cone again, the silly sods!" Williams yelled.

In the trucks the riflemen thrust their weapons through the holes in the canvas and started to blaze away, as the Arabs came racing in on their camels, crouched low, their robes flying in the breeze, their long antiquated rifles balanced on the beasts' humps.

An Arab came tumbling down to the sand, as his camel raced on without him. Another was hit but remained lolling in his saddle.

"Aim at the broadest spot on the camel!" Williams, their marksman, yelled above the angry snap-and-crack of the small arms battle. "Then you'll hit something at least." Next instant he put his own theory into practice. Without seeming to aim, he pulled his trigger. A great scarlet stain appeared on the right flank of one of the racing beasts. It went down on its hindlegs immediately, snorting with pain, sending its rider flying. He ran back and started belabouring the wounded camel with his whip. Calmly Sergeant Williams took aim and shot the Arab neatly through the head. "Try that one on for size, mate," he said, pleased with himself.

Next moment the riders had turned and were flying

back the way they had come, leaving four or five of their number, littering the desert like abandoned rag dolls, Hard couldn't help thinking.

They pushed on.

Now the character of the desert started to change, as the exhausted men, grateful that the sun was finally beginning to sink, staggered on. The sand was now broken up by patches of scrubby camel thorn and what looked like grass. A few hundred yards further and they saw it really *was* grass: poor, yellow parched stuff, but grass all the same. The soft wind which was now blowing over the desert was not the usual blistering hateful thing of the interior. This breeze was fresh and cool. Hard's spirits leapt. They were coming to the sea.

Turning to the Professor, who lumbered on behind him carrying two of the exhausted foot-sloggers' rifles over his massive shoulders, he croaked, "Not much further now, sir. We're getting close to the sea."

"Thank God for that," Professor Challenger boomed. "The men have about had it."

Hard nodded numbly and slogged on.

Ten minutes later the Arabs appeared on their camels at about thousand yards' distance away, just out of rifle range. But this time, starkly outlined, in the blood-red light of the dying sun, they did not come charging, whooping crazily and waving their weapons. Instead they simply sat there on their mounts, occasionally pointing at the little convoy, but otherwise motionless. There was something sinister, eerie, even frightening about their postures and Sergeant Williams bringing up the rear of the men on foot, snorted angrily, "I wish them Wogs would sling their frigging hooks. They're getting on my wick just sitting like that."

As if in response to his wish, they did just that a few minutes later. They turned their camels and disappeared over the dune noisely like black ghosts.

Hard asked himself if they had gone for good? Had they perhaps failed to find the Germans, without whom they would not attack in strength? Perhaps they had contacted them, but perhaps the Germans had too much on their hands at Tobruk at this moment to bother with a handful of stragglers? But even as he told himself this, he knew he was wrong. The Germans and their treacherous Egyptian allies had been on to them right from the start in Cairo. They wouldn't let them get away, if they could stop them. He told himself they would only be safe when they were on board Lt Christian's old tub – what had he called it? The "Mucky Duck". Yes, on board her and heading for Gib as fast as she would sail – then they'd be safe . . .

Ten miles away at sea, Lieutenant Christian allowed himself a small tot and then went up to the bridge. For an old man CPO Thirsk seemed tireless. He was still at the wheel after all these hours. He must have the stamina of a horse. "Do you want me to take over now, Chiefie?" Christian asked gruffly. "Then you can go to your bunk and get your head down for a bit."

"No sir. But thank you all the same," Thirsk replied, eyeing the darkening sky gratefully. "I'll wait till it's properly dark and then I'll go off watch. I imagine we'll be all right then."

"All right, Chiefie," Christian said eyeing the dull pink hue of the horizon to port. "That'll be Tobruk over there. Judging by those fires, it must have taken some stick. I wonder how long it'll take the Jerries to capture it— " He stopped short and cocked his head to one side. "What's that?" he asked startled.

Thirsk did the same. "Aircraft engines," he concluded after a moment.

Together they stared around the horizon. Far away just barely visible in the quickly darkening sky, Christian saw them – a flight of three aircraft heading south in a metal V. "Jerries, no doubt," he said with grim humour, "about to honour us soon with their presence."

"Fuck it!" Thirsk exploded, cursing violently, something which was unusual for him, "aren't we going to be spared nothing?"

Christian patted the old petty officer on his skinny shoulder. "I'm afraid we're not, Chiefie. But we'll survive. We have to, don't we?"

Numbly CPO Thirsk nodded his agreement.

They ploughed on through the dark sea, with the aircraft getting closer by the second . . .

The German halftrack came nosing its way over the dunes, just as the sun vanished altogether, leaving the desert a sudden inky-black. But for a moment it was visible, then it was gone. But the rumble of its rusty tracks was still clearly audible.

Hard made a quick decision. "Out of the truck – all of you. Move it!"

Shocked by the new danger, they fell out of the back while Hard ran to the cab. "Dickie," he snapped to Bird, "fix the accelerator – wedge it or something – so that the Bedford keeps on going."

"Sir," Dickie Bird understood immediately. In the darkness the enemy halftrack would be listening for the sound of the vehicle, which obviously would have been reported to them by the marauding Arabs.

Hurriedly Hard collected his little troop together. In an urgent whisper, he said, "Not a sound. No lights either.

Keep close up. Anyone who lags behind will have to look after himself. We're not turning back for stragglers. Got it?"

They murmured their assent.

"Dr Stein you stick to me, Professor Challenger you bring up the rear with Sergeant Williams here."

"The truck's ready, sir," Dickie Bird cut in.

"Good man. Get it moving then."

Bird hurried back to the cab, depressed the piece of wood he had used to jam the accelerator, slammed home first gear and flung himself out of the open door, as the Bedford started to move off down the rough track.

Hard waited till he was clear before whispering, "All right, off we go. Head for that glinting light. That's the Mediterranean." They needed no urging. The night was suddenly cool and the new danger and fear pumped fresh adrenalin into their tired bodies. They set off at once.

Hard, in the lead, flashed a look over his shoulder. The three-tonner was jolting on at five or six miles an hour, its ruptured engine making a racket. It would be loud enough, Hard hoped, for the Jerries in the halftrack to hear it and home in on the empty vehicle. With a bit of luck it might give them thirty minutes or so respite, enough time to get into the rocks and boulders of the rendezvous site. There, again with luck, they might be able to hold off the Germans till Christian appeared with his battered "Mucky Duck".

"Famous last words," a cynical little voice rasped at the back of his brain, but Hard, already panting with the effort of fast marching, ignored that unpleasant little voice.

SEVEN

"That's them," von Almaszy said. "That's their truck."
He dug the driver of the big halfgrack packed with his
Brandenburgers, in the ribs. "After it."

The Afrikakorps man rammed home the huge gear
lever and the armoured vehicle started to rumbled forward
once more, heading in the direction of the engine noise.
Behind in the armoured rear the Brandenburgers, all tough
adventurous young men, slipped the safety catches off
their weapons and prepared for the killing to come.

In the cab, von Almaszy half raised himself and peered
into the inky gloom. He would have liked to take the
English alive, especially those two mysterious civilians
they had with them, but he wasn't going risk his young
men's lives. In the confusion of a night fire fight, more
people than necessary could get hurt. They'd fire first and
ask questions afterwards, he decided.

The laboured noise of an engine in difficulties grew
louder. They were close now. He narrowed his eyes to
slits and peered even more intensively through the gloom.
Then there it was a big square English lorry ambling along
somewhat crazily, as if the driver had had a few more
drinks than necessary, bumping against the petrol cans
which lined the track and zig-zagging from left to right.

The driver of the halftrack knew what to do. He was

one of Rommel's veterans. He slewed the big armoured vehicle round so that it was now running parallel with the slow-moving truck at perhaps a hundred metres' distance.

Von Almaszy raised his voice above the roar of the engines and the clatter of the halftrack, *"Feuer!"* he bellowed.

Lining the left side of the halftrack, his Brandenburgers opened fire with a will. Tracer sped towards the truck. At that range even the poorest shot couldn't miss and they were all skilled marksmen. Slugs peppered the whole length of the Bedford. Von Almaszy tensed himself for answering fire. Surprisingly enough none came. All that happened was that one of the truck's rear tyres exploded like a bomb. Next moment, the Bedford was plodding on, bobbing up and down awkwardly like a man who had injured his ankle.

"Heaven, arse and cloudburst!" one of his troopers cried in exasperation. He raised himself to his full height. Out of the side of his jackboots he plucked a stick grenade. He grunted and then threw it at the truck with all his strength.

It landed squarely to the right side of the truck, just behind the driver's cab. The impact raised the heavy vehicle from the track. Next moment in the flash of angry red flame, the Bedford slammed down again and came to a stop, sagging badly to one side, as its rear ankle snapped.

"We've got them," von Almaszy shouted in triumph. *"Los Jungs. An den Angriff!"*

The Brandenburgers needed no urging. They vaulted over the side of the moving halftracks effortlessly and doubled forward, firing from the hip as they ran. But still no answering fire came from the disabled truck. Had the grenade dealt with the English, von Almaszy asked himself as his young troopers doubled forward, their firing dying away as they realised they were meeting no opposition and were simply wasting ammunition.

In a curved skirmish line the young soldiers advanced on the truck, its engine still running. Still there was no answering fire from it. Von Almaszy pushed his peaked cap to the back of his head in bewilderment. What was going on? He knew Hard and his gangtsters. They should have started shooting now. Their very lives were at stake, weren't they?

A minute later he learned he had been tricked when the Brandenburger sergeant who had discovered the accelerator had been wedged and that there was no driver in the truck – and no good English cigarettes to loot either – yelled, "There's no one here, sir. The Tommies have pissed in our boots!"

Von Almaszy did not waste any time in cursing. The English couldn't be far away. He knew that from the Arabs. But it was pitch black and the desert was big. He raised his flare pistol and pulled the trigger. A red flare sailed into the sky effortlessly and exploded with a faint plop, bathing the area in a ruddy unreal glowing light. It was the signal for the Arabs.

They appeared from nowhere. Their dark, hook-nosed faces rapacious and eager for loot, as he gave them their orders, making a gesture with his thumb and forefinger as if he were counting money, one that they knew well, and brought an even greedier look to their dark, evil eyes. Von Almansy told himself they'd slit their mother's throat for a Maria Theresa thaler. Then they were gone, whacking the sides of their camels with their whips. Von Almasy nodded his satisfaction. If anyone could find the damned Tommies, it would be the Sensussi riders . . .

Hard heard the boom of the German grenade and knew that it had to be the enemy. "All right, lads," he called softly to his men, "stand to. It won't be long now."

The men, chilled now by the cold breeze which came in from the sea behind them, lifted their weapons and stared expectantly into the darkness. Hard had formed a small perimeter, perhaps fifty yards in length, behind a row of jagged boulders, with the little deep water estuary to its centre. Once – *if*, a little voice queried at the back of his mind – the "Mucky Duck" arrived, the two flanks would fall back and embark, while the centre held till they were safely on board. Then the centre – he, Sergeant Williams and Professor Challenger – would make a run for it, covered by the fire of those already on board. But where was the damned tug?

While the men were preparing themselves for what might come, Hard walked over to Dr Stein and said, "Dr Stein, I've got a job for you, if you would take it."

Lisa was scared but she didn't show it. She couldn't, not with these brave young men who were risking their lives in the attempt to save her and Professor Challenger. "Anything," she said immediately.

Hard forced a weary smile, though she could hardly see the smile in the darkness. He gave her the big torch, the only thing he had taken when they had abandoned the truck. "Come on over here."

Carefully they wended their way through the boulders until he again located the little cavelike structure at the water's edge – perhaps once in more peaceful days, some Arab fisherman had used it as a shelter.

"Now if you would," he suggested, "I'd like you to

position yourself here where you can't be seen from the land and as soon as I've gone start signalling out to sea at ten minute intervals."

She flashed a quick beam of light around the little cave with its sandy floor and wet dripping rock walls. She didn't like the place one bit, but she knew she couldn't refuse the young officer. "What is the signal?" she asked.

"Very simple," he answered. "The morse code SOS – save our souls. Like this." He crept into the cave and flashed the code quickly. "Do you think you can manage it?"

She forced a laugh, "Well, if the product of twelve years of expensive university education can't, then we might as well, as you English say, shut up the shop."

She laughed and he did too.

"All right," Hard said, "then I'll leave you here. You'll be OK, won't you? Of course, if you don't— "

"Don't go on so, Major Hard," she interrupted him. "I can manage quite well."

"Fine." He went and for a moment she crouched there, suddenly feeling very lonely and afraid. She pulled herself together and entered the cave which felt as cold as the grave. She shuddered and sat down. Then as an afterthought she pulled out the little pistol, placed it on the rock beside her and stared at the green glowing dial of her wristwatch waiting for the first ten minutes to pass when she would flash her signal.

Time passed leadenly. A sickle moon had risen now, casting its silver spectral light over the sea, tinting the slight waves an icy hue. She had sent the signal once and then again, straining hard to spot an answer to the signal. In vain. The horizon had remained obstinately empty. It

190

almost seemed as if she were alone in this cold night world, the last person alive. Again she shuddered.

At ten she sent the SOS signal once more. This time she thought there was a response. Faintly on the horizon she saw a light. It seemed to be in the sky rather than on the water. She stared hard. Yes, she was sure she had seen something. Then it was gone.

Her first impulse was to run and inform Hard. But she realised she had to stick it out and give another signal. This time she would be more positive about what she saw if the tug responded. So she waited, cold and shivering in the damp little cave.

She glanced at her wrist-watch yet again. The ten minutes seem to take an incredibly long time to pass. Suddenly she started. There was a strange crawling noise coming from the wet sand close to the sea. She bit back her scream. Was it a snake? She couldn't recall whether were snakes in this part of the Western Desert. There it was again. A furtive, hesitant movement on the wet shingle. She felt a cold finger of fear trace its way icily down the small of her back. Almost unconsciously she reached out and gripped the little ivory-handled pistol she had been given at Tobruk. There was something out there. It wasn't a snake. It was too big for that. She knew, too, that whatever it was, it meant harm to them. Why else this furtive approach?

Silently she clicked off the safety catch and raised the pistol. Her hand was trembling badly and she had never fired a gun in her life before. But she had to now. She had to raise the alarm if necessary.

Then there it was. It was no animal. It was an Arab, crawling on all fours, coming out from between the rocks, his hawk-nosed raffish face briefly illuminated in the cold silver light of the sickle moon. In his teeth the Arab carried a curved knife, which glittered in the moonlight. Instinctively she knew his aim was to plunge it into the back of one of the unsuspecting Englishmen defending the perimeter. She counted to three and pulled the trigger.

The gun jerked violently. A spurt of scarlet flame stabbed the glowing darkness. The knife clattered to the shingle from the Arab's teeth. The next moment he screamed piteously and fell on his back, knees raised, writhing and thrashing around in the wet sand, screaming hideously.

That single shot acted like a signal. Suddenly firing broke out everywhere and there were hoarse cries of rage, fear and anger, as the fire fight commenced.

EIGHT

Christian was now at the wheel, while Thirsk tried to get some sleep, though the former doubted that CPO, who worried like a mother hen, would get any. For an hour now the enemy fighter bombers had been searching for the "Mucky Duck". Time and time again they had come close to locating her, dropping their great bundles of flares which illuminated the sea for yards around with their ghastly, unreal silver light. But so far the tug had been lucky.

Holding the wheel, Christian popped his head outside the wheelhouse and listened hard. Yes, there was another of the sods, droning around somewhere overhead. The sound of the plane's motors was faint, but definitely there.

Christian moved his head back inside and frowned hard. Would their luck hold? he asked. Now they were off the coast, ready to pick up the Hard party, the last thing he wanted was a dive bomber attack. Trapped in the little natural harbour he'd be a sitting duck. The Jerries would have him on a silver platter.

The door to the wheelhouse opened. It was Thirsk. He had a steaming mug in his right hand. "Couldn't get any kip, sir," he said awkwardly. "So I had a quick shufti around the "Mucky Duck". The lads are all at their stations. And the cook sends up this. Char with a dash of Nelson's blood."

Christian grinned in spite of his worries, "Oh Chiefie, you are a real old clucking hen. Thanks all the same." With his free hand, he accepted the mug and had a sip of the scalding hot tea and rum. "That hits the spot," he said appreciatively.

"That's what Cookie thought, too," Thirsk said.

Despite his toughness, Christian felt a glow of emotional warmth for his crew: ordinary young men living a tough, dangerous life under terrible conditions, more often than not living off cold rations, the high spot of their day, a *Woodbine* and a tot of "Nelson's blood". Yet they were so loyal and worried. He shook his head and a close observer could have seen a momentary sheen in his red-rimmed eyes.

"There's something going on on the shore," Thrisk broke into his reverie. "Can you see, sir?"

Christian could. A mile or so away, the silver darkness was broken by a pattern of tracer and the sullen red flashes of what might be exploding grenades. "It's them," Christian said, draining his mug. "I'm sure of it." He jerked the telegraph and, after whistling into the tube, said to the engineer, "Give me what you can, Scottie. We've spotted them."

Apparently the pilot of the German plane, trying to find the "Mucky Duck", had too. For suddenly the noise of aircraft motors grew louder and by craning their necks in the wheelhouse, the two of them could see the dark shape of a plane heading straight for the scene of the fire fight.

A minute later the first of a series of bundled flares came sailing down to illuminate the stretch of coastline in stark icy silver light.

"To judge by the firing," Christian said, "it looks as if Hard's lot have formed a perimeter around the anchorage. The Jerries, by the looks of those muzzle flashes, must be attacking in strength. Chiefie, we've got to get them off tootsweet. They won't be able to fight off that lot much longer. It's going to be nip and tuck."

"I've already issued the Tommy guns to the on-duty watch, air."

"Good for you. But we'd better sound action stations. When we go in, we want every man with some sort of weapon. The brown jobs will need all the fire support we can give them."

"Ay, ay, sir," Thirsk agreed and went out, but at the door of the wheelhouse, he paused and said urgently, "but what about the Jerry plane?" He indicated the dark shape in the sky dropping yet more flares.

"God knows." Let's worry about that sod when we get that far. Now sound action stations . . .

The single light'German mortar fired again. There was a loud plop, the sound of metal rattling in a tube, an obscene belch and another mortar bomb whizzed through the air. It exploded right to the front of the perimeter. A huge smoke hole appeared suddenly like the work of some gigantic mole. Hard frowned. He knew what the Germans were up to. They were ranging in. Once they had the defenders cowering behind their boulders, they'd rush the perimeter.

Up above the plane continued to drone round in circles, dropping flares. Obviously the pilot was uncertain about what was going on. So he did nothing. But Hard guessed once the "Mucky Duck" appeared, he'd know which side to attack.

"Here they come!" Williams yelled at the other end of the perimeter.

"Stand to," Hard bellowed. "Fire at will. *Fire!*"

The Brandenburgers came in a rush, firing from the hip as they did so. With them were their Arab allies on foot now and carrying the Mausers the Germans had given them as a reward for their scouting. In German and Arabic they cried their war cries, carried away by the crazy blood lust of battle.

"Luvverly grub!" Guardsman Smith yelled above the racket, and squinting along the barrel of his Lee-Enfield, he started pumping shots at their attackers, as calmly as if he were back at some peacetime range, trying to qualify for his marksman's badge.

That first volley crashed into the Brandenburgers with murderous effect. It tore great holes in their ranks. Men went down everywhere. The lieutenant in the lead clutched frantically at his chest. His legs buckled under him slowly. He fought off death. His hair hung down, blond and shining in the light of the flares, like that of a capless schoolboy. To no avail. Death took him. He pitched face forward into the blood-red sand, dead before he hit the ground.

All about him his men yelled, shrieked, crying out in their sudden agony, pressing home their attack, the attack slowing godown, as if they were suddenly moving through thick mud which clutched and gripped at their ankles. Still they came on and Williams came running up back to centre where his position was, crying, "The flanks will hold, sir. But we've got to stop them here!"

"Never fear," Challenger boomed, pumping shot after shot into the Germans, as if he were back as a teenager in the trenches in the old war when the spike-helmeted Prussian Guards had attacked. "We shall hold them."

And he was right. Just twenty metres or so short of the

British positions the Germans broke. In front the Arabs, wailing like crazy things, turned and ran, throwing away their weapons in their haste to get away from that deadly fire. Moments later the Brandenburgers followed. But they faced the enemy as they did so, pulling back slowly, firing aimed shots to left and right, with some of them trying to drag their lightly wounded with them.

"Cease firing!" Hard yelled, as Guardsman Smith and Williams continued systematically to pick off the retreating Germans, their faces set and hard and exhibiting no pity. Indeed, Williams shouted, without taking his eyes off his front. "Let's finish as many of the squareheaded sods off as we can . . . they'll be back."

"Conserve your ammo," Hard countered angrily, for already he was aware of the flashing light from the sea which indicated the "Mucky Duck" was coming in. "We'll need every bullet we've got before this business is over . . . *Cease firing!*"

Von Almaszy was angry. He turned to the Brandenburger, in leather face mask and goggles, and snapped. "You need not be afraid. You'll be covered by the halftrack until we're right up to the Tommies' positions. Then the driver will swing the halftrack round so that you have its armoured protection in front of you. You'll fire from the other side of the vehicle. Do you understand?"

"*Jawohl, Herr Hauptmann,*" the Brandenburger answered, his voice muffled and distorted strangely by the face mask.

"You'll be flanked by two riflemen. They'll give you protection if needs be. But I don't think that will be necessary. *Klar?*"

"*Klar, Herr Hauptmann,*" the man replied.

"All right then, get to it."

With difficulty the man swung the heavy pack, attached to the tube, over his shoulders, watched a little nervously by his flank guards. They knew what a fearsome weapon the masked man was going to employ. But it could backfire, they knew that, too, and they could just as well be the victims as the Tommies some 200 metres away.

Von Almaszy slapped the steel side of the halftrack. The driver recognised the signal. He started up. "As slow as possible," von Almaszy shouted above the noise of the engine.

With a rusty squeak, the half track began to move off. Behind came the masked man with that hideous weapon balanced on his back and his two apprehensive flank guards, both with their rifles at the ready. Von Almaszy nodded his approval grimly, as they vanished into the silver darkness. That'd settle the Tommies' hash, he told himself. In a few minutes they'd come running out, with their hands in the air pleading to be allowed to surrender. Then he'd take his revenge . . .

There it was, Lisa Stein recognised the signal at once. It was the SOS they had been waiting for for so long. Ignoring the dead Arab sprawled out dramatically in the extravagant pose of those put to death violently, she stepped out of the damp cave and flashed her own signal. She waited tensely, half conscious that some heavy vehicle was moving towards the perimeter. The answer came – another flash of swift morse. *They had seen her signal!*

She waited no longer. Hurriedly she stowed the torch in her pocket and ran half-crouched, to the centre of the perimeter to where the Professor, Hard and Sergeant Williams sprawled in the sand, facing the unseen enemy. She flopped down beside them and gasped, "They're coming in. They've seen my signal and they're coming in."

"Jolly good," Challenger exclaimed.

"Thank Christ for that," Hard breathed out gratefully. "Sarge," he turned, "alert the two flanks, will you?"

"Yessir," With his rifle at the trail, bent low, Williams doubled away to spread the good news.

But the momentary smile of relief which had crossed Hard's face vanished to be replaced by the same worried look as before. "They're up to something," he whispered, head cocked slightly to one side as the noise of a motor running at very slow speed came ever closer.

"What do you think is going on, Major?" Challenger asked.

The flare which came sailing down from the circling plane in that very same instant gave the big academic his answer. It exploded in a burst of glowing incandescent white light, turning night into day, to reveal the halftrack and the three men behind it, advancing on the perimeter with dread purpose.

Lisa's hand flew to her mouth in fear. "What's . . . what's that man in the mask?" she asked in a tiny voice.

"I'll tell you," Challenger said before Hard could reply "I have seen it before back in '17 when I was a boy in the trenches on the Western Front. It's a flame-thrower."

She gasped with shock, while Hard lying next to her remembered that horrible day that summer in the 1920s when he had burst in on Mr Ryan unexpectedly. Mr Ryan, a kind, middle-aged man, who often gave him boiled sweets, always wore a black bandage round the top of his head. When Hard had asked his father why, the reply was always, "Mr Ryan got hurt in the big war . . ." or "He was badly injured in the last show." But on that hot

199

July afternoon when he had run through the open french windows he had learned the nature of Mr Ryan's injuries – and they were horrific.

Mr Ryan had been busily engaged in removing the long black bandage and he had stood there in the sunlight watching with terrified fascination as a completely bald head had been revealed, wrinkled and lobster pink, flecked with patches of brown. Later in his mind's eye he would compare it with those of the thousand-year-old mummies he would see in the British Museum. But it was a little lower down that he had spotted the thing which had given him nightmares for months afterwards. *Mr Ryan had no ears.* Where they had been there was nothing but two dark holes from which the yellow wax had oozed unhindered. Later when he had calmed down, his father had sat him on his knee and had told him that Mr Ryan's ears had been burned off by something called a flame-thrower.

Now here in this remote place, he was facing up to that weapon he had dreaded ever since that July day so long ago . . .

NINE

"Sound actions stations!" Thirsk yelled.

The klaxons and the alarm bells shrilled and jingled, as the "Mucky Duck" started to slow down to enter the narrow harbour. For a moment they drowned out the crackle of small arms fire, but when they stopped, CPO Thirsk had to make himself heard by shouting hoarsely, "Oerlikon guns closed up?"

"Ay ay, Chiefie," came back the reply.

One by one the gunners answered, "Brownings closed up . . . Holman Projector closed up . . ."

Thirsk turned and reported "All closed up," to Christian, leaning out of the door of the wheelhouse, judging the width of the anchorage.

"Thank you, Chiefie," Christian said hastily and went back, while the crew members who were not manning the guns took up their positions, armed with the American Tommy guns. "All right shore party," Thirsk snapped, as the tug slowed down even more. "This has got to be done at the double. Off sharpish and over the brown jobs. Then back on board again – also right sharpish." He cast an eagle eye down the rank of young ratings, feeling that same old excitement he had felt first as a boy at the Battle of Jutland in 1916. "Now then, get yer fingers out. We're about there."

Up at the wheel, Christian ordered, "Engine room – dead slow – both."

The "Mucky Duck" was moving now at a snail's pace and Christian knew that once the German plane somewhere up above spotted them, they'd be in for trouble. They'd have to move with the utmost speed to get out of this death trap, in which there was no room to manoeuvre. But he'd worry about that later, he told himself. First he had to get the brown jobs and the civvies aboard.

Suddenly he was startled by a great whooshing sound like some primaeval monster drawing in air. He looked to his front. A long ugly stick of angry red flame, tinged with an oily yellow hue, had shot out of nowhere. "What in God's name is that?" he stuttered. "I've never seen anything like it." Then he remembered. He had seen something similar on an old pre-war newsreel of the fighting in Spain. "Hell's teeth," he said in horror, "the Hun's using a flame thrower . . .!"

"Williams," Hard ordered, as that first terrifying rod of flame vanished. "Get to the right flank. Start moving them to the boat."

"But sir—"

"No buts," Hard cut him off brutally. "Move. We can manage without you."

Reluctantly and crouched low, Williams doubled away to carry out the order.

To their front the carrier was moving once more. Now it was less than a hundred yards away, which Hard guessed would be the right range for the terrifying weapon of war. "Professor," he said, hardly recognising his own voice, "you follow."

"I'm damned if I will," Challenger retorted sharply. "I

202

faced up to those things before. They don't scare me. That man carrying the flame-thrower is highly vulnerable. If you knock him over he won't be able to get up again with that weight on his back – and if you hit the backpack, he'll fry to a cinder."

"All right, have it your way," Hard gave in. "Here they come again. Let's see if we can't get him underneath the halftrack. Here they come." Again the driver slowed the vehicle round and braked in order to provide cover for the three Brandenburgers. Abruptly there was a great hushed intake of air. A tongue of oil-tinged flame shot out. In its path the sand shrank and turned black. Before their terrified gaze the boulders to both sides turned an ugly glowing purple. The flame dropped short, but the heat was terrifying. It dragged the air from their lungs, making them cough and splutter, gasping for breath.

Hard felt the bile rise in his throat. He could have vomited on the spot, but he knew he had to keep control of himself. "Fire now," he said thickly.

The two them fired hurriedly trying to hit the man's legs underneath the halftrack as he recharged his terrible weapon. To no avail. The halftrack started to move again and they knew they had failed.

Hard flung a glance to the right. Dark shapes were hurrying aboard the tug, but there were still a dozen men on the other flank to be evacuated. It would take another five minutes and the way things were he knew they in the centre couldn't last more than a couple of minutes at the most.

Again that awesome flame licked out greedily, trying to reach them like that of some predatory, prehistoric monster blindly searching for its prey. The heat almost engulfed them. There was the stench of burning. Hard could feel his hair being singed.

Suddenly he snapped. The next time they would die. Why not die now if he had to die?

"I'm not having it!" he yelled aloud. Before Challenger could stop him, he had risen to his feet and clambered on top of the nearest boulder. Here he had the advantage of height. He fired without appearing to aim. The driver of the halftrack slumped over the wheel of his vehicle. Next moment the vehicle's engine stalled and it came to an abrupt stop. Slugs started to cut the air all around the lone Englishman. Hard staggered as one slammed into his left arm.

"Kill him," von Almaszy yelled above the racket. "He's the leader . . . *Kill him!*"

The man with the flame-thrower raised his nozzle. He was supremely confident now. The Tommies had not been able to hit him. There was nothing the defenders could do against him. He'd flame the man on the rock and then he'd do the rest. Slowly, almost pleasurably, his forefinger curled around the big trigger.

Hard fired first. The bullet hit the German, whose top half was visible from the rock, squarely in the chest. In the instant of the impact, the German swung round, finger tightening on his trigger with the shock. The flame shot out. Von Almaszy screamed as it engulfed him, tearing at his flesh devouring it greedily and even as he died his flesh bubbling and smoking, his nostrils were assailed with the stench of charring skin.

The Brandenburgers panicked. They shrank back following the Arabs, who were wailing and praying to Allah at the same time. Hard didn't wait for them to rally, as

German troops always did. Despite his exhaustion – it felt as if a tap had been opened and every last bit of energy had drained from his body – he dropped from the rock, grabbed Challenger's big paw and cried, "For Christ's sake, let's go!" Then they were running all out for the "Mucky Duck".

Christian rang the telegraph. "Slow ahead both," he commanded. On the shore the Germans had recovered and were pouring a hail of fire at the departing tug, which Thirsk's shore party were returning with their tommy guns. Tracer zipped back and forth lethally and the Germans had already set up their small mortar and were about to bring it into action.

The "Mucky Duck"'s engines throbbed and Christian tried to ignore the wild shooting match, concentrating on getting the old tub through the narrows and into the open sea beyond. He knew the danger now came not from the Germans on shore but from the plane which was still circling, dropping flares. As soon as they were clear, Christian knew the German would come in on a strafing run. Already his anti-aircraft gunners had begun firing a protective barrage. But so far they hadn't hit the damned German plane.

On deck, a harassed Hard ordered Challenger and Dr Stein to lie down. He could have sent them below he knew, but in case they were bombed he thought they would be safer on deck as long as they were not standing upright. Pistol in hand he snapped off shots to left and right, keeping the Brandenburgers ducking behind the boulders which lined the shore. But already they were beginning to diminish in size as the "Mucky Duck" drew away with ever increasing speed. So, in the end, as the firing began to die away, he thrust his pistol back in its holster and tensed ready for the new danger – the one from the air.

It came just as the tug started to clear the harbour. At zero feet the German fighter-bomber came hurtling in through the silver night, cannon chattering frantically. White tracer shells zipped lethally at them. The radio mast was hit. It came tumbling down in a mess of tangled wires and sparkling cables. A jagged line of holes ran the length of the funnels. On the deck a sailor screamed, high and hysterical like a woman, and sat down suddenly, staring dully at his severed leg which lay on the bloody deck next to him, as if he couldn't understand how it had got there.

With a terrific burst of speed, the German plane soared into the sky. But an angry, apprehensive Hard knew it would be back. The target was too tempting, too easy. "Stand by to abandon ship, lads!" he called as a precaution.

"I can't swim," Dickie Bird wailed plaintively.

"Well now's the frigging time to learn, Dickie," Guardsman Smith sneered, "cos— "

The rest of his words were drowned by the roar of the Messerschmitt's engine as it came in for another run.

"Here comes the sod again," Thirsk yelled above the racket, as the gunners swung their weapons round to meet the challenge once more. Over at the rocket projector, Bunts, who had been assigned to the strange ugly-looking weapon by Thirsk, tensed. "Bleeding useless thing," his "oppo" Sparks had sneered. Now he'd show Sparks.

Again the fighter-bomber came in skimming over the surface of the sea its prop. lashed the sea just below its evil blue belly into a white frenzy. The pilot pressed his firing button. The four cannon burst into vicious life. Once more a stream of white glowing cannon shells converged on the slow-moving tug. They ripped jagged holes the length of the superstructure. The wheelhouse was hit. A lifeboat was riddled and reduced to matchwood. And all the while, the Chicago pianos and Oerlikins pumped a desperate stream of fire at their attacker. But the German seemed to bear a charmed life. With desperate courage he pressed home his attack, seeming to slide through that terrible wall of fire. Another mast went, as did another lifeboat, its derrick shattered by shellfire so that the riddled boat dangled over the side, half in the water.

Bunts waited no longer. He pressed the trigger. The two rockets shot into the air, trailing red angry sparks behind them. They spread out to left and right. A thin tangle of steel wires were just visible in the silver light.

Then it happened. The attacking plane ran straight into the wire. They caught at once. Its prop was seized and stopped immediately. Desperately the pilot tried to fight the crippled plane to land on the shore. To no avail! Suddenly its yellow-painted nose dipped alarmingly. He threw back the canopy. Too late. The fighter slammed into the rocks at 400mph. It disintegrated in a great burst of yellow flame, metal flying everywhere in a glistening silver rain, as on the deck of the battered "Mucky Duck", the exhausted men cheered and cheered. They had done it . . .!

Christian died half an hour later. They had found him slumped on the debris-littered floor of the shattered wheelhouse, moments after the German plane had been shot down. Thirsk and Hard had rushed in to tell him the exciting news, only to discover him slumped over the wheel. He had still been conscious, but barely. Blood was jetting from a great gaping hole in the small of his back, through which they could see the shattered bones glistening like polished ivory.

Desperately Hard had tried to staunch the flow of blood with a shell dressing, but the bandage had been soaked and useless within seconds.

They had propped him up half-doubled in a chair in a hope that this might help, but he had continued to bleed, his breath becoming shallower and more hectic by the instant. "Cara," he had gasped more than once. Then he had attempted to get to his feet, gasping, "Close up gun crews . . . come on now, look lively." Gently they had lowered him to the blood-soaked chair, his eyelashes flickering and the eyes themselves threatening to roll upwards all the time. "I once gave a tart seven and a tanner to do it in an airraid shelter in the Hedon Road," he choked. "Right old knee-trembler . . ."

"He's virtually gone now, sir," Thirsk had whispered, tears glistening in his old eyes.

Hard had nodded, but said nothing. It was almost all over, he could see that, too. He had seen enough men die in this war; he knew the signs. He looked at Christian's ashen face and wondered if he were still fighting death or whether he *wanted* to go.

"Poor old "Mucky Duck"," Christian had said quite clearly, then his head had lolled to one side and he was dead.

"Poor old "Mucky Duck"," Hard had echoed the words quietly, while the tears had streamed down Thirsk's wizened face. He had reached over. Gently he closed Christian's eyes. The escape from Tobruk was over.

Envoi

FROM LADY LISA CHALLENGER, OBE

Duncan Harding has asked me to write a little afterword. If it helps to honour the memory of those brave young men, who helped to rescue us from Tobruk, and my dear husband Professor Challenger, who was killed by a V-2 missile in the last months of the war, I am proud to do so.

They are all long dead now, of course. The "brown jobs", as they were called by the crew of the *Black Swan*, died young – in Italy, France, Germany and later, Burma. As for the Navy men, including "Chiefie" Thirsk, they went down when they were torpedoed in the English Channel one winter's night in 1944. None of them survived.

But there *are* many old men in both Britain and America still walking around today who would have died violently fifty years ago, if it had not been for the efforts of those brave young men in that June of 1942. By saving my dear husband and myself, they helped, indirectly, in the production and success of the atomic bomb.

I know it is fashionable these days, so long after the grim times of the war, to regard Japan as the victim and America as the aggressor when that latter country dropped the first atom bomb on Hiroshima. It is also often stated that we dropped the bomb on the Japanese

211

because they were Orientals and, therefore, inferior. But that is simply not true. Our political and military leaders would also have dropped the bomb on the Germans if they had not surrendered in May 1945. Time had been running out fast for the Nazis that year, especially after the camps had been discovered. I can assure you of that.

Hiroshima was bombed not to set an example, but as a final warning to the Japanese military and people. In that same week of May when peace came to Europe, on the Pacific island of Okinawa alone, the Americans were losing a thousand men a day to the fanatical Japanese defenders. After Okinawa would come Kyusha, the defence of which was being planned by the Japanese army command based at Hiroshima. Then would come the other main Japanese islands, one by one.

At that time there were four million Japanese soldiers and armed civilians in Japan, plus 4000 Kamikaze sui-cide planes waiting for the expected Anglo-American invasion; and everyone connected with that invasion anticipated terrible casualties. Throughout America, hos-pitals had been cleared for the wounded and injured. The US Chief of Staff told President Truman, who would make the decision to drop the bomb, America alone could expect half a million casualties. That was the reason the bomb was dropped.

Today, as a very old lady, I read and hear of the too many revisionist historians who are trying to rewrite the history of World War Two. These revisionists have not "risked their necks", as my dear husband used to say. They have never been shot at, been scared out of their wits, starved, undergone terrible privations for a "cause", which could – and often did – result in their dying violently. What would they know of the motives of young men like

212

Major Hard, or Lt Christian and all those sailors with their funny nicknames, "Bunts", "Sparks" and the like? They died probably unwillingly, dead before they had begun to live, for something they believed in, fighting against an enemy they believed implacable and brutal. I believe we should leave those brave young men their honour, don't you? Let the honoured dead rest in peace . . .

Lisa Challenger,
Queens Blvd,
Forest Hills,
New York
Spring 1995